RV, having successfully completed his freshman year at the demanding Boston Latin School, is hoping for a great summer. He's now fifteen years old and looking forward to sharing many languid summer days with his friend Bobby, who's told him he has gay feelings too. But life and family and duties for a son of immigrant parents makes it difficult to steal time away with Bobby.

Bobby, too, has pressures. He spends part of the summer away at football camp, and his father pushes him to work a summer job at a friend's accounting firm. Bobby takes the job grudgingly, wanting to spend any extra time practicing the necessary skills to make Latin's varsity football team.

On top of everything, RV's best friend Carole goes away for the summer, jumping at an opportunity to spend it with her father in Paris. Luckily, there is always Mr. Aniso, RV's Latin teacher, to talk to whenever RV is lonely. He's also there for RV when he inadvertently spills one of Bobby's secrets, and Bobby is so angry RV is afraid he is ready to cut off the friendship.

WHY CAN'T FRESHMAN SUMMER BE LIKE PIZZA?

The Pizza Chronicles, Book Two

Andy V. Roamer

A NineStar Press Publication

www.ninestarpress.com

Why Can't Freshman Summer Be Like Pizza?

Printed in the USA

Print ISBN: 978-1-64890-021-1

First Edition, June, 2020

Also available in eBook, ISBN: 978-1-64890-020-4

WARNING: This book contains gun violence, racial slurs, sexual assault (on page), graphic violence (knife attack), and drug use.

For Rimas, who shared growing up with me, in celebration of the summers we spent watching those wonderfully terrible movies at the drive-in.

Chapter One

Summer Solstice

I used to love summer. The long, languid days. No school. No homework. Sleeping late. Going to the beach. Staying out later in the evenings and watching the sun set over the hills into the darkening glow of the horizon.

Wow. Am I starting to sound like a poet or just a pretentious a-hole? What's wrong with the paragraph I just wrote? There are no pretentious words in it, are there? Well, maybe "languid" is. I like "languid." I don't know where I picked it up, but I think it perfectly describes summer. Where everything is a little more s-l-l-o-o-w-w-w and easygoing. Where life seems good and there's no homework. Yup, I'll stick with languid. Hey, there has to be a benefit to liking words the way I do. I'm not just a nerd, but a poetic nerd.

Ha ha ha. Maybe it has something to do with being bilingual. I never used to think about it much before, but I guess I am officially bilingual. Talking Lithuanian at home. English in the outside world. Just kind of always accepted it, didn't I? But I wonder what speaking two languages does to someone. Kind of like being split into two people. My Lith life and my English life. Are there really two people inside me? Scary thought. One of me is bad enough.

Luckily, Bobby Marshall doesn't seem to be bothered by it, so why should I be?

Ahh, Bobby Marshall. I still can't believe we're friends. Or should I say "special friends"? I'm still afraid to even think about it. Me, RV Aleksandravičius—nerd extraordinaire, spawn of Lithuanian immigrants, word lover, nervous worrywuss, possible gay person—friends with one of the biggest jocks in school. The world truly is an amazing place.

But, as I was saying, I *used to* love summer. That was before I had to work. This summer I'll be toiling away like the rest of humanity. And I'm not just talking about working with the Computer Fix-It company I started last year with Carole. That business has been kind of rocky lately. I'll blame it on the bad economy, since everyone always blames everything on a bad economy.

No, I'm working at my first real job. I turned fifteen last week. I used to love my birthdays. The end of school. The start of summer. But not anymore. Dad has a friend at work, Mr. Timmons, whose brother, Ed, owns a garage and gas station. Dad was talking to him and lo and behold (another pretentious choice of words?), Mr. Timmons told him his brother was looking for someone to help with chores around the place. Since I'm not sixteen yet, I'm not supposed to work in the garage itself. But I can dispense gas and work around the store that Ed has attached to the garage. Nothing heavy duty, Mr. Timmons said. Ed just needs someone fifteen to twenty hours a week helping in the store and cleaning around the place. A great way to earn a little pocket money.

Fifteen to twenty hours! Dad, bless his parental heart, volunteered me. Said it was a great way to learn about "real" life. And to "round out my skills." What, my skills are too flat or something? But Dad doesn't stop. "Too much time with your nose in a book isn't healthy." "Develop some skills." "A young man needs more than book learning." On and on and on. Says it in the Mother Tongue, of course, but that's how it translates into English.

Except it sounds more serious in Lithuanian. *"Per daug laiko praleidi su nosim knygose." "Išmok ką nors naudingo." "Jaunam vyrui ne tik knygos naudingos."* Wonder why that is. Because it's what we talk at home? Our "real" language? To Mom and Dad, English sure isn't real. Even though they speak it, Mom much better than Dad. What is real to me, then?

Oh, well. In whatever language, I think Dad wants to have a macho son like the other guys at work brag about. Well, sorry, Dad, not all of us can be macho. And not all of us can be like Bobby Marshall either. A jock. Smart. And nice. Yeah, nice. He likes me. I still can't believe it sometimes. He says I'm fine the way I am. Okay, Bobby, if you say so. I'll believe you. I *have* to believe you. Have to believe someone likes me the way I am.

Oh, RV, stop feeling sorry for yourself. There are people who like you besides Bobby. Mom, for example, though Mom doesn't really count because moms usually love their kids no matter how screwed up they are. But then there's Mr. Aniso, my Latin teacher last year. Good old Mr. Aniso. He's been great, especially when I've told him my worries about being gay. We're becoming real friends. But he's an adult. Adults only go so far for a kid. We need our peers to like us.

So what about Carole? You've gone through a lot with her, RV, and she's still sticking by you. Yeah, that's true. She's a good egg. No, a great egg! I love you, Carole Higginbottom!

And what about Ray? Brothers are usually close, aren't they? But not Ray and I. Too bad. He's just off in another world. I'm sure he thinks it's a cooler world than the one his nerdy older brother inhabits.

So there's Bobby. He's a guy. A regular guy. Something I've always wanted to be, but will never be, alas! (Another one of those words! Where are all these pretentious words coming from?). Anyway, if Bobby really likes me that would be amazing. I still can't believe it happened.

There I am thinking about him again. But that's okay, right? I mean, after all, we kissed and everything.

!!$$#*&!! Did I just write that? Yes. GET OVER YOURSELF, RV! YOU KISSED A GUY AND YOU LIKED IT. What's wrong with that? You're not hearing thunder from heaven, are you? This computer isn't blowing up because you wrote those words, is it? So you might be gay. Chill out. Or you might be bi. After all, you enjoyed making out with Carole until she started falling for that zit-faced Tim— Whoa! *Whoa!*

I have to stop worrying about everything. Maybe Dad's right. Maybe too much time on the keyboard, writing down my thoughts, isn't good. But I like keeping this journal. Helps me sort things out. When Mom and Dad gave me this computer they said they wanted me to make good use of it. I think I have. Maybe not the way they'd want me to, but I think they'd be proud of me for writing so much. And I kept it up all school year. That's good, isn't it? Even if Mom and Dad would be shocked at some of the stuff I wrote here. I hope I keep up the writing during the summer. After all, I should have more time in summer, even if those languid days are cut by fifteen to twenty hours a week.

*

I gotta go! Bobby just called. He has some free time and asked if I want to get together. Of course I do. He told me he wants to take me to a special place he's discovered. A quiet place where he can think and dream. I showed him the special place in the woods behind the ball field in West Roxbury, where we live, but he says he has another one, maybe better. Okay, we'll see. I could use as many of those places as I can find. Places to forget work. Or being macho. Or pleasing other people. Sounds just like what I'll need this summer. Okay, Bobby. Here I come!

*

Funny how circumstances can change your outlook on things. The place Bobby has discovered is in Larz Anderson Park. In Brookline, next to West Roxbury. It's a pretty enough park, I suppose, with a cute lake and trees and flowers, and even an auto museum with some cool old cars. We've gone there on a couple of occasions as a family and had a good enough time.

But I'll always remember the skating rink. It's not enclosed like other rinks are, so if you're a good skater you can enjoy doing your pirouettes on the ice while looking out at the snowy landscape or the starry sky. (Pirouettes. Why do some words sound prissy?)

Anyway, I said if you're a good skater. I wasn't, though Dad kept taking me, trying to get me to learn. "*Čiuožk! Nebijok nukristi! Čiuožk!*" Dad's way of motivating me. "Just skate! Don't worry about falling! Just skate!" Like so many things, it didn't work. After about the fourth or fifth time of going and falling, I landed smack on my nose and almost broke it. Since then, Dad and I have avoided the park like the plague. But Dad keeps trying, doesn't he? Like telling me to cut down on the books. I guess he hasn't totally given up on me being more like the sons of his friends at work.

But going there with Bobby is a whole different story. It took us a while to get there on our bikes since Brookline is pretty big. I was a little nervous whether I could keep up with Bobby since he's such a jock and in great shape, but I did okay. And, yeah, he did stop a couple of times so I could catch up with him, but he didn't make a big deal of it or anything. Maybe that's what I like about him most of all. He never makes me feel bad about anything. Though he could. Man, he really could!

Anyway, it was already late in the afternoon when we got there, and I was pretty sweaty after cycling in the hot sun. So we locked up our bikes and cooled down, walking around the lake and through the trees.

We ended up on top of a hill, the skyline of Boston visible in the distance.

"Nice view, eh?" Bobby said, grinning. "As good as your place by the stream in the woods?"

"Yes!" I exclaimed. With the tall, shiny buildings reflecting the sun, Boston looked like a magical city outlined against the bright-blue sky. The park around us felt like some kind of magical place too. Some people were trying to fly kites in the gentle breeze. Other people were on blankets having picnics. And others were sitting or lying on the grass doing nothing or just holding hands and talking quietly. Everyone seemed happy. Yeah, summer! It makes me happy too.

Bobby still grinned at me. "But this still isn't the special place I wanted to show you."

"No?"

"No. Follow me."

He led me to some trees on the side of the hill. They formed a little grove, a private place where you were hidden from everybody else.

"But when you sit down here, by this tree," Bobby said, doing just that, "you can still see out. But you're pretty much hidden from view."

I sat down next to him. Yes, there was Boston through a small break in the trees. And there were all the other people on the hill, enjoying what they were doing, totally oblivious to our existence. (Oblivious is a good word too. It's a little like invisible, but better. It means you do exist, but are clueless. Hello! How often do I feel clueless about things?)

Bobby and I sat there for a while, not saying anything, just enjoying being together, feeling like we were watching the whole world but not letting the world see us.

"So? Was this worth the bike ride and the climb?" Bobby finally asked.

"You bet. I love finding special places. Like the place in the woods not far from my house. It's a good place to think and dream."

Bobby nodded. "Yeah. I discovered this spot when I came to the park with my folks. They just wanted to sit and relax on the hill, so I went exploring."

"Yes, exploring is good. Where would we be in life without exploring!"

I laughed and gave Bobby a nudge. He nudged me back. "Now I've shown you a good place to think and dream too."

I nodded, and we sat quietly for a long time, just happy looking out at Boston and being next to each other. Bobby put his hand on mine and it reminded me again of the first time he had touched me in the spring. The crazy, amazing feeling that went through my whole body. I know it's stupid to say, but it was like I became alive in a new way. Even though that jolt of excitement lasted only a few seconds, I'll never forget it.

It was great to experience the feeling again. Bobby's gentle touch on my hand probably didn't mean much to him, but to me it meant a lot, especially that things were good between us. It was one of those moments in life when everything seems perfect. Just the way it's supposed to be. I wanted to stay there forever with Bobby's hand on mine.

Then I remembered something. "Hey, Bobby!" I exclaimed, turning to him.

"What?"

"It's the summer solstice!"

Bobby looked puzzled.

"The longest day of the year. When the sun is exactly over the Tropic of Cancer. It happens every year between June 20 and 22. And this year it's today."

Bobby suddenly laughed. "Oh, RV. You should go on a game show!"

My cheeks were getting hot. Carole calls it the RV Blush. When I'm really embarrassed about something, my face turns bright-red. And I was really embarrassed by my nerd part coming out in front of Bobby of all people.

Bobby was still laughing. "I believe you. I really do." He put his arm around me and gave me a little hug. "Being with you, I learn all these crazy things. That's why I like you."

"Don't these long days make you feel good?" I said, more quietly. "Summer stretching out ahead. It makes me feel optimistic. Like I'll have time to live my life, and not just do homework. Or chores. Or other things I'm forced to do. Summer is for us."

I don't know if it was because of my long speech or something else, but when I glanced over at Bobby again, his happy expression had changed. He seemed somewhere else, thinking about something.

"We might have to give in to some things we have to do," I said, "like my working at Ed's Garage, and stuff you have to do. But that's okay. We're going to have a good summer anyway. Right?" I kept talking, not wanting Bobby to give in to whatever was bothering him.

"Right."

But Bobby didn't sound too confident. And the frown was still there on his face.

Bobby told me he'll be going to football camp later in the summer. It won't be for all summer, but I wondered if he was having second thoughts about it.

"C'mon, we really are going to have some fun, aren't we?" I repeated, again trying to make him forget whatever serious thoughts were on his mind. "Summer's a great time. Even if we'll be busy, me in the garage and you at football camp. We'll still have time for some fun, right?"

"Yeah, sure." Bobby still had the same look on his face.

I had to find out what was on his mind. "Bobby, what's the matter? Is everything okay?"

"I'm sorry." He shook his head a little. "I'll be real busy this summer. I think it's all good stuff. But, still, I don't know if I'm happy about it or not."

"Don't you want to go to football camp?"

"Oh, I—yeah, a lot. But there's something else. I didn't have a chance to tell you."

"What?"

"I'm going to be doing some work too."

"I thought the program your dad was trying to get you into didn't work out?"

Bobby's dad is as bad as mine. Trying to get him into all sorts of programs at the bank where he works even though Bobby is only in high school. But his dad's ambitious. And he wants Bobby to be ambitious too. I guess that's one way Bobby's like me. He's not sure if he wants to follow in his father's footsteps.

"Well, Dad doesn't give up. He talked to as many people as he could, and something opened up with one of his friends. Joe Moocher. He's an accountant, who has his own business. Dad says this is a great opportunity to see how accounting works up close. And he says it's not too many hours and won't interfere with the football. So I can't say no."

"Our fathers need some parenting lessons, don't they?" I said, trying to keep things light. "Lay off your sons!"

Bobby didn't laugh.

"Do all fathers want their sons to be exactly like them?" I asked, turning a little more serious myself.

Bobby ignored my question. "It's not like I don't want a good career," he said, obviously still thinking about the job with the accountant. "It's just that—it's just that I don't know what career I want." He continued talking, still thinking about everything he'd told me. "I wish my parents would leave me alone. I wish that everything I do wasn't so important to them."

I didn't know what to say, but it got me thinking about my parents too. Was everything I did so important to them the way everything Bobby did was important to his parents?

Bobby had started talking about his father. "It's like he wants me to fight all the crap he had to fight in life. But I want him to let me live my life and deal with my own crap."

"I'm sorry for all the pressure you're feeling," I said, full of sympathy for him. "I feel pressure too."

"At least you have a brother. I'm the only kid. I think it makes it even worse."

"Yeah," I agreed, "though Ray seems about as different from me as a brother can be."

Bobby let out a laugh. "Me, working with numbers!" he exclaimed. "If you think my writing and spelling needs help," he added, shaking his head, "you should see my math homework."

"Is accounting all about math?"

"I think so, but I don't know. And I don't know if I want to know." Bobby grew serious again and stared out through the trees. "I just wish I could be more sure about things." He turned to me. "And then there's the gay stuff. Some days I feel the crap just doesn't stop."

"I know." I nodded. "The gay stuff gets to me too. Sometimes I think it's a big deal and other times I think it's not a big deal at all. And shouldn't be."

"I know what you're saying." Bobby sounded glum. "But it's a big deal for me. The last extra thing I need to worry about. My father, the football team, the coaches." He turned to me, his expression stern. "Promise me you're not going to say anything to anybody about us, RV."

"Okay." I nodded again.

"No. Promise me, RV. It's really important to me."

"I promise."

We sat there in silence. Was the gay stuff a big deal or wasn't it? I couldn't answer that question, but I had to respect Bobby's wishes. I told myself I didn't know the first thing about what it was like to be a football player, so I had to follow Bobby's lead.

Bobby's hand rested on the ground and I placed mine on top of his. It was my way of telling him I would keep his promise. And maybe more. Sitting there, with my hand on top of his, made me believe a little more that things would turn out all right. That he and I together could fight whatever crap the world might throw at us.

"It's okay, Bobby," I murmured. "We'll still find time for us. And you'll figure things out."

Bobby took my hand and gave it a little squeeze—his way, I hope, of telling me he agreed with me. But I could see his mind was still on the coming summer he might not have.

So I didn't say anything more. We stayed quiet, just looking out at Boston through the trees, lost in our own thoughts.

We sat in silence for a long time and finally realized it was getting late when some lights started to come on in the distance.

Bobby was still looking a little sad, so I had to try one more time. "I love these long, languid summer evenings," I said, throwing in my favorite word of the moment. "Don't the lights turning on make you feel like life is good. That magic is still possible?"

A grin appeared back on Bobby's face. "Languid? Where did you get that word, RV?"

"I don't know. I just like it."

"I like it too." Bobby removed his hand from my hand but then patted it instead. "You and your words, RV," he said smiling. "Keep 'em coming."

"Are you sure?"

"Yes. I like them."

"Really?"

"Really."

We sat there for a long time, enjoying the languid summer evening. In that moment, it seemed as if magic was really possible. One way or another we'd be able to solve whatever problems might come our way.

*

Magic doesn't last long, though, does it? By the time we pedaled home it was totally dark, and I got a talking-to from Mom and Dad. More like a yelling-to. They were getting so worried, they said. I could have had an accident, they said. "I'm sorry. I'm sorry," I said in return. Glad Dad didn't threaten me with his belt tonight, like he used to when we were small. Luckily, he's finally realized you don't do that to your teenage son. Nor to my twelve-year-old brother, who will be thirteen soon. Though he can't help pointing to his belt sometimes. One of his New World gripes. *"Man nesvarbu jeigu to nedaro Amerikoj. Darė kur aš gimiau."* "I don't care if they don't do that in America. They did that where I grew up."

Oh, well. Will Dad ever mellow? Who knows? After sitting there with Bobby on top of that hill, sharing a quiet moment, whatever crap my parents throw my way won't bother me.

Chapter Two

The Disappearing Summer

I can see keeping summer as great as it used to be, is going to be harder than I thought. Mom and Dad are still on my back, ready to snatch more summer away from me.

It's not enough that I'll be working fifteen to twenty hours every week at Ed's Garage. Mom and Dad are determined to get me into more Lith organizations and go to Lith camp this summer.

Mom, being the good, religious woman, is pushing me to go to a camp sponsored by a Catholic religious organization, the Futurists. Sounds a little scary if you ask me. Actually, I've belonged to the *Ateitininkai* since I was a little kid. That's the actual name of the organization. It was founded more than a hundred years ago when the Old Country was ruled by the Russians. The things Futurists believe in aren't bad: God, country, family, and living through Christ. That's their motto.

I guess the Liths needed the *Ateitininkai* to get rid of the Russians, but is it really necessary now? I mean, I don't know if I believe in God, but I try to live through Christ. Usually. Sometimes? But we don't need to get rid of the Russians now, just keep them out of our elections, right? Besides, what am I going to do at a camp run by priests and nuns?

Dad's pushing me go to camp, too, not with the Futurists but with the Boy Scouts. I have nothing against nature and running around in the woods, but it's the people who I don't particularly like. Not the Boston Lith scouts anyway. They're more into drinking and smoking and making out in the woods, instead of enjoying nature. They're the cool kids. Not my thing. I'll never be cool, no matter how hard I try. And I've already been called a few names by those guys, names I'd rather not remember. Can I help it if I like to read and dream instead of smoke and drink? I don't think the guys at scout camp would take too kindly to me—to put it mildly, ha ha.

I don't know what it is. Why are Mom and Dad so concerned with Lith life for me and my brother, Ray? Aren't they happy enough that I went to Lith school every Saturday for years when we were in grammar school? Didn't I get enough lessons about our immigrant heritage and tradition? I think Mom's more willing to let go of the past. But not Dad. He even lectured me the other day about a speech the Dalai Lama made somewhere where he said if you neglect your traditions, you neglect part of yourself. Great. So now I'm supposed to be like the Dalai Lama. It never ends.

Jeez, guys. Can you give me a break and let me be a normal kid for a few minutes? Can't I concentrate on my life—my life which is in America? At least for the summer? That life is complicated enough as it is.

Right now it looks like the chances of me having a normal summer are about as good as me becoming a jock or learning to speak Chinese. Mom and Dad are just too much into wanting me to be better than just your normal, average kid. I guess I'm a lot like Bobby in that respect. My parents want me to be something, but maybe something that means more to them than me.

I think there's another reason Mom and Dad are so into Lith life these days. They're making a final push to get their US citizenship. They've had their green cards for a long time—too long if you listen to Mom. Dad's been the one who's hesitating more. He still has sisters and cousins in the Old Country, while Mom doesn't, not close relatives anyway. Sometimes when Dad gets mad he talks about moving back there.

Maybe that's why he's held back. Giving up his old citizenship represents some kind of big change or break with his family. His old family, Mom calls them. She keeps reminding him he has a new family here. Though she hasn't gotten her citizenship either. She says she's been waiting for him so they become US citizens together. I wonder. Maybe she's a little afraid of the big break too.

Whatever it is, they both swear they're both finally ready now. Time to give up those old passports. Embrace the new life. Go USA! Fine, so do it! I'm sick of hearing about the Old Country. I have my current country to worry about.

Luckily, today I had enough energy to fight Mom and Dad to a draw. They won't force me to go to Lith camp—for the moment. To be discussed in the future, as they say in Washington's negotiations. Man, is everything going to be politics from now on? Why does life take so much energy? So I'm going to spend the summer fighting to stand my ground with Mom and Dad instead of having fun?

That's what summer is supposed to be, right? Fun. Relaxation. A break from life's responsibilities. But between Bobby's parents and mine, getting those breaks will be tricky.

Ah, Bobby. Why do I like him so much? Because he's nice to me? Yeah, but other people are nice to me. Because he's a jock, and jocks aren't usually nice to me? Maybe. But it can't be just that. He's special, at least to me. And I can't stop thinking about him. And I want to be with him. So does that mean I have a crush on him?

A crush. What a stupid word. It sounds so infantile and flighty, like something not to be taken seriously. Something little kids have. What I feel for Bobby is serious. I wish I could explain it, but I can't. I just know Bobby means a lot to me. And he's a guy, so does that mean I'm gay?

But doesn't Carol mean a lot to me? Yes. And she's a girl. And didn't I have a crush on her? So what does that mean? I'm not gay? Bi, maybe? Or was I just trying to prove something with Carol? Kind of like pushing myself when I spent time with her, even though Bobby was always in the back of my mind.

Man, I have to stop. These questions are going to drive me crazy. I've got to learn to relax and let go of the Lith stuff. And the sex stuff. I have a big day tomorrow. My first day at Ed's Garage. That's going to be fun, ha ha. Why couldn't I come up with my own job so Dad couldn't push me into this one?

*

Well, it wasn't such a bad day after all. I survived my first stint at Ed's. Not that it was paradise. More like purgatory, if not quite the place with the devils. Ed, the owner, seems like a nice enough guy. He said my duties will be to help him clean up, help pump gas, fetch stuff, and maybe even help him with some paperwork.

Yeah, he used the word fetch, like I'm a dog or something. Oh, well, sometimes I think I was a dog in a previous life, so this fits. Wonder what kind of dog I was, though. I'd like to believe I was a bulldog or a German shepherd. But more likely I was some kind of mutt. As long as I wasn't a poodle or one of those femmy dogs with pointy snouts and no fur.

Anyway, Ed's is part garage, part store, part gas station. It's like any other Mom and Pop place, a little bit of everything to make money where you can. The building looks pretty run down so I guess making money hasn't been all that easy for Ed. The white part—or what used to be white—looks kind of beat up and needs a good coat of paint. That might be one of my jobs. Ed told me he might want to paint the place later this summer. That I don't mind. I've painted enough for Dad, and it's never seemed like a chore. And call me weird, but I even kind of like the smell of paint.

But for now it's business as usual. And there's enough of it. Customers like coming here because Ed is so friendly. He's round and fat and waddles like a duck. But he chats everybody up and makes jokes, so I guess customers get some entertainment through their car windows while their gas is being pumped. And they'll pay a little more for that even though there's a self-service place not too far down the road.

I'm taking notes for my computer business with Carol and Tim. We haven't had too many customers lately, so I wonder if people would like it if we made jokes while fixing their software or setting up their new computers. "Better run, Mrs. Jones! Your hard drive is about to explode!" "Mr. Peebles, watch what you're saying. There's a microphone in your motherboard. The Russians are listening!" "Mr. and Mrs. Anderson, you might be victims of identity theft. How much money do you have left in the bank?"

Just kidding, folks!

On second thought, I'm not sure if people would appreciate the jokes. They're pretty serious and cranky when their computers give them trouble.

One thing at the garage isn't funny. Very *unfunny*, in fact. Melissa. She's Ed's assistant. She's fat too. But she doesn't crack jokes or waddle. She's stern. And she marches and talks fast. Talk about serious! Her face is always red like she's ready to blow her stack any minute. Glad the garage is officially off-limits for me. That's Melissa's territory, and she can have it.

I already got into trouble when she was showing me around. I bumped into a shelf and knocked some tools and rags down onto the garage floor. She turned even more red and I thought she was about to blow her stack.

"Watch it, RV!" she shouted and then she calmed down a little. "This place might look disorganized. But it's not. Everything has its place." She gave me a stern look before instructing me to help her pick everything up and put it in its place.

When we were done putting everything back, she asked, "How are you around engines?"

"Not very good," I answered. "Dad told me Ed didn't need another mechanic. Besides, I'm not supposed to work in the garage since I'm only fifteen years old."

"Okay. Good. Because I'm the other mechanic. Forget I asked," Melissa said with a weird smile—her version of trying to be nice, I guess. "The store and outside is your territory. The garage is my territory."

"Yes, ma'am." I felt like saluting her.

Melissa continued with her instructions. "Most of the time, we need someone to help answer phones, look after shelves, clean up stuff, and maybe even run the cash register. I do that now, too, but sometimes I get too busy." She gave me another one of her don't-mess-with-me looks. "And don't even think about helping yourself to what's in the cash register. I have ways of keeping track of all that."

I bet she did. I had a vision of reaching into the till and a huge axe coming down from somewhere and chopping my hand off.

Today they had me move some junk that was in the back and throw it in a dumpster by the side of the road. I also had to sweep and clean. All in all, nothing I couldn't handle. As long as I stay out of Melissa's way, I think I'll be okay.

*

First Bobby's parents, then my parents, and now Carol. The crap keeps coming! What a bummer!

It's Sunday. We went to church and there was no Ed's Garage today. So I thought I'd see if Bobby was around. But he was busy with his folks. Then Carole called.

"RV, can you meet me at Joe's?"

"Okay."

"I have something to tell you."

I was hoping it wasn't bad news. Carole's already had a tough few months with her parents deciding to split up, so I was afraid more bad news would send her over the edge. I knew I'd be able to tell as soon as I saw her face. Carole is like what's her name with the Greeks and Trojans, the woman whose face launched a thousand ships. Helen. Carole's face launches a thousand emotions.

I hopped on my bike and went off to Joe's Pizza, glad that Carole wanted to confide in me. It's good we're friends again. It was touch and go there for a while, when she started going out with Tim and didn't tell me. But all is forgiven. And I have to remember, I haven't told her about Bobby, have I, since he made me promise not to tell anybody he might be gay.

Someday I'll tell her, and when I do, I hope she'll understand why I had to keep Bobby's secret. A secret is a secret, right? And promises friends make to each other have to be honored, right? Even from other good friends.

I was the first one to arrive, so I got my pepperoni slice and sat in my favorite booth. Good old Joe's. The place where Bobby and I first used to meet. The other kids from school don't go there much, even though I think the pizza's really good. So it's pretty private. And Joe is great. He doesn't bother us. Lets us sit there for as long as we want. So it's a great place to get away from home when Mom and Dad are arguing. Or just to have a slice and hang out.

If only life could always be like Joe's. Well, maybe that's asking for too much. How about summers? Yeah. Forget life. Don't want to be selfish. How about just summers?

"Hi, RV."

I must have been daydreaming big time because I didn't notice Carole come in. She sat down, and I was glad to see her face didn't look sad. Not by a long shot. She bounced with excitement, not at all upset.

"RV, guess what?"

"What?"

"I'm going to Paris!"

"*What*?"

"I'm going to Paris!"

"Really?"

"Yes. Really."

"Wow." I sat back in my seat. "So tell me. How did this happen?"

"The army is sending my father to Paris to work on some project with the French. He's leaving next week. And he called Mom and asked her if I could join him for the summer. At first Mom hesitated, but he convinced her it would be a great opportunity for me, so she said yes."

"How long will you go for?" I was already missing Carole.

She shook her head. "I don't know. We haven't worked out the details yet. Much of the summer, I guess."

"Wow." That's about all I was able to say—again. "Wow. Wow. Wow."

"I know. It's so exciting, isn't it?" Carole stood up, and I thought she was about to start dancing right there in the middle of Joe's. But she bowed instead. "*Enchanté. Comment vous appelez-vous? Je m'appelle Carole.*" She burst into giggles so loud, other customers looked over at her.

But she was so happy, she didn't care. "*Mais oui! Je suis trés enchanté!*" She started her French again, sounding just like an actress I heard in a movie once. She sat back down. "I've been practicing already."

I was growing sadder and sadder, thinking about a summer without Carole. Who would I complain to if I had a fight with Bobby? Or what if he got even busier, and wouldn't have time to see me, despite his promises?

"What's the matter?" Carole asked. "Aren't you happy for me?"

"Sure," I said. "But I'll miss our talks."

"It's not like I'm going away forever." Carole tried to sound reassuring. "And it's not like they don't have cell phones in Paris. And there's What'sApp."

"Yes, true." But I probably didn't look as if I believed her.

"RV, don't worry! I'm not going to Mars. And I'll be back." Carole wasn't about to let any negative thoughts spoil her good mood. And who could blame her?

At this point, I was really, really tempted to tell her about Bobby. After all, it seemed like it wouldn't be so bad. She'd be far away, on another continent, so it wouldn't be as if I was breaking my promise to Bobby. Not really. Or would it?

But I didn't. I don't know what stopped me. The Big Guy upstairs? I still don't know for sure if I believe in Him, so why is He so often on my mind? One of those unfathomable questions of life. "Un-fath-om-ahh-bull." Great word. Kind of wraps around your tongue, not to mention your brain. Like life, I suppose. Because in the end you can't figure it out, and you get all tangled up in yourself if you try.

"So what do you think, RV?"

"Huh?"

"RV, you weren't even listening to me." Carole looked upset.

"Oh, I'm sorry," I apologized quickly. "I—I was just thinking how I'd miss you."

"No you weren't."

"Yes, I was."

Carole gave me one of those I-know-better looks, but luckily decided to let it drop. "I was saying," she began again, pronouncing each word slowly, "that we shouldn't let the computer business go. Can you work with Tim to keep things going?"

"Uh, sure."

"RV! I really mean it! Tim has some really good ideas for growing the business, and you should have more time during the summer."

"Don't be so sure," I said. I told her about my first day at Ed's Garage and Melissa.

"RV the mechanic." Carole giggled. "Has a nice ring to it."

"Thanks a lot. You'll be in Paris, and I'll be sweeping floors and running away from Melissa."

"Hey, RV! Maybe I'll meet some enchanting French gay guys, and I can invite them here to meet you. Or better yet, you can visit me there! Hey, that's an idea! Wouldn't that be great?"

"Yeah, sure. How much gas do I have to pump to pay for the airfare?"

*

I took a detour instead of going home after seeing Carole. Went to my favorite spot in the woods behind the ball field. Not quite as exciting as the spot in Larz Anderson Park Bobby took me to, but still a good place to think and relax. I think of it as my place. The place I showed Carole. Then Bobby. So I guess a place for all of us.

I went to my favorite spot on the rock near the stream and sat there, looking out over the hills in the distance. Sat for a long time, trying to calm down. I was thinking, about nothing in particular, just letting the thoughts come and go. Thought about Bobby. And missing Carole. And bossy Melissa at the garage. Started to feel sad. Don't know why exactly.

Is it about missing Carole? A little. But I think it's more than that. Maybe it's about summer and all the crap that's threatening to make it not so fun. Yeah, maybe that's it. I feel like my summer is being taken away from me. Mom and Dad wanting me to go to camp and get back to Lith life, Carole leaving, Bobby's parents pushing him to do stuff he doesn't want to do either. Then there's the gay stuff. What happened to summers like they used to be, when I didn't have to worry about all this crap?

*

And another nail in the coffin of my summer!

I spent the afternoon with Tim on our first computer job together. I suppose Carole brought him on board to our computer business because he knows so much about all kinds of machines. Knowledge is great, but could it be too much of a good thing? I should have been clued in that there might be trouble when I went over to Tim's house the other day. He spent forever showing me the new computer his parents bought, talking about techie details I have no clue about. Do I really care about the wonders of his fancy new graphics card or SSD drive?

I tried to say things that made me sound excited and knowledgeable. "Oh, great, Tim." "Yeah, those pixels really pop, don't they?" "The speed of five gigahertz per second is so cool!" But when Tim started talking about some kind of HexaCore processor, my eyes really started glazing over.

We spent the afternoon hooking up a new computer for a new customer. Tim didn't let me off the hook, giving me commands all the time.

"No, no, RV. Give me the Ethernet cable, not the USB cable!"

"Not that one, RV! This one! That's the modem!"

"C'mon, RV! What's the matter? The cable should be easy to plug in!"

Mrs. Winslow is the new customer. She's a widow who lives a couple of blocks away and saw our notice at the supermarket. She's a nice lady but so nervous about everything. "Be careful! Don't hurt yourself! Watch the lamp! Are you sure it's safe?" Between her nervousness and Tim's bossiness, I thought I would lose it.

There's another thing. Mrs. Winslow not only wants her new computer hooked up, she asked if we could give her some lessons.

If she drives me crazy, what's bossy Tim going to be like when Mrs. Winslow starts asking basic questions? "Why did my screen go dark?" "What does this light mean?" "Why did everything suddenly disappear?" "I swear I didn't do anything! The computer did it itself!"

I think we'll have to charge extra for clients like Mrs. W. And maybe I'll need some calming down.

At least I didn't have to squeeze into any tight places with Tim the way I did with Carole. That would have been really bad. I probably would have decided to quit right there and then. I came close to doing that when we went back to Tim's house. We were trying to come up with a plan to get more customers for the summer. Tim's all about going on Facebook and Twitter and other websites to drum up business. I told him people who go on those sites already know about computers and don't need our services. We have to do things the old-fashioned way, by leaving notes on bulletin boards of stores and putting up flyers. I reminded him about Mrs. W, who found our note at the supermarket.

Tim told me that's my job. As if he's my boss. He used to be a nice enough guy. What happened? Are computers turning him into some kind of techno monster? I wanted to text Carole and complain, but then stopped myself. Don't want to bother her with these petty problems while she's dreaming about going up the Eiffel Tower or flirting with some handsome French guy.

So I guess I'll just suck it up—for now anyway. I have a lot of other things to think about. Dealing with Tim is the least of them. Here I was, excited about the start of summer and it's turning into something that's making me feel bad, not good. Why does life work like that?

Chapter Three

Being Selfish

"RV, I need to see you."

Bobby was on the phone.

"Is everything okay?"

"Yeah. Yeah. I just need to chill out. And you're my friend for chilling out."

We decided to meet at Joe's. As I made my way there, I wondered if Joe would want to start charging me rent at some point. Or maybe a therapy fee or something. He's nice and all and never bothers us. But I was just there with Carole. And now Bobby. I hope as long as we keep buying slices and Cokes Joe is okay with me being a constant presence in his pizzeria.

"So, what happened?" I asked Bobby when we were both settled in a booth and eating our slices. Bobby was very upset, hardly making eye contact with me. I could tell he was lost in his own thoughts again.

"I had a bad fight with my father," he said, finally looking up.

"What was it about?"

"The usual. Time. My time. That accountant, Joe Moocher, wants me to work too many hours. It will really cut into my football practice. And forget about having any free time."

"And your father's agreeing with him?"

"Yeah. I told my father it was just too much. One thing led to another, and we ended up yelling at each other."

"Usually those things blow over, no?"

Bobby shook his head. "I don't know. We both said some pretty crazy things. I called my father a reverse racist for feeling we needed to prove all these things to the White Man."

"I'm sure he didn't like that."

"No. He called me an ungrateful, spoiled brat. Asked me if I had any idea how much he had to go through to get that VP position at his job." Bobby let out a laugh, but it was anything but joyful. He continued, mimicking his dad. "Do you know how much shit I needed to eat, Bobby? Do you?" He pushed aside his pizza slice and kept repeating in a singsong voice, "Do you know how much shit I needed to eat? Do you know how much shit I needed to eat?" Then his voice grew louder. "Well, too bad, Dad! Because guess what? I need to eat my own shit. I need to eat my own shit!" Bobby kept saying it louder and louder until a few customers turned to stare at us.

He noticed them gaping at us and stopped. "Sorry, RV. You can see I'm all wound up. I apologize."

I nodded, not being sure what I should say.

But Bobby was still upset. "Maybe I should just apologize to everybody," he started saying, a little more quietly. "Apologize to these people. To my parents. To the whole world. Ha ha ha. Would that make everyone happy?"

"Apologize for what?"

Bobby shook his head. "I was just kidding. I don't need to apologize to anybody, and you don't either, RV. We don't need to apologize to anybody." He was quieter now, but I could see he was still upset. He looked at me. "RV, do you think it's selfish?"

"What is selfish?"

"Just to want to live your life and not worry about anybody else?"

"Why should it be selfish?"

"I don't know. Look at all the people marching and trying to change things to make the world a better place."

"I'm just trying to figure out where I fit in the world first."

That made Bobby laugh. "Oh, RV. I love it when you say profound things. Knowledgeable and profound."

"That was profound?"

"Sure." Bobby punched me playfully in the shoulder again. "Know thyself. Doesn't it say that in the Bible?"

"I'm not a big Bible person. Catholics usually aren't. We listen to the Pope."

"But Protestants are Bible people. My mother knows it backwards and forwards. She leads a choir and teaches Sunday School. What a woman!"

Bobby made some more comments about his parents being very accomplished. Parents whose standards he could never live up to. But he looked happier, not as upset as he was earlier.

I reminded him what he said about not apologizing for anything.

He was smiling at me. "You're right, RV. See? I know it was a good idea to call you. I feel better already."

He kept smiling at me. Seeing him so much happier made me happy too. I remembered the time Bobby put my hand to his face to prove to me he was blushing, even though I couldn't see it. I had an urge to touch his face again.

Bobby confronted me. "Why are you blushing, RV?"

I was? That made me blush even more. "I don't know."

"What, RV? What?"

Sometimes I think Bobby can tell what's on my mind before I can. Like Carole. It's crazy. And wonderful. The memory of touching Bobby's face was stronger than ever.

"RV. You're blushing like crazy. What's the matter?"

"Nothing."

"Don't give me that."

"I don't know why I'm blushing." Sometimes one has to lie. No, maybe it wasn't really a lie. Just a little fib. Since it was partially true. "I—I'm just glad we can talk the way we do. It makes me feel good to be with you."

"It makes me feel good to be with you too." Then Bobby turned serious again. "RV, I'm sorry again for losing it earlier. I feel really bad about it. But sometimes I can't help it."

"Are you going to try and make up with your father?"

"Of course. And that won't be easy either. But I do get where he's coming from. Making it big as a black man is not easy, though people don't want to hear about it. But still, I don't like it when my dad and I fight like that. It's terrible."

I nodded. "Yeah. I hate it when my parents argue. That's why I come here so often. When they argue, the atmosphere at home is hard to take."

Bobby agreed. "Yes. It's good to have a place to come to. And it's good to have a friend to talk to about these things."

We sat there for a long time, neither of us wanting to leave. By the time we did go, it was late. I wondered if I'd get another lecture from my parents. Whether I did or not didn't seem to matter much tonight. I was glad I could be there for Bobby. I understand parents worry about things like being home before dark or letting them know where their kid is. I get it. But I wish they also understood why it's necessary to break those rules, sometimes. And lay off the lecture.

And what do you know? I got off easy tonight with just a few questions. Sometimes I wonder if Mom and Dad can read my mind too. Can't I get away with anything? Why have a password on this computer then? Might as well let them see it all. No. Maybe this is one place I can really call my own. The only place I can keep any secrets.

*

I couldn't fall asleep for the longest time last night. And when I did I had another crazy dream. It was another one of my roller coaster dreams. Bobby was on a roller coaster in the first car, without any other passengers on it. I was on the roller coaster behind his. There were no other people on mine, either. Both our coasters started moving, with Bobby in front and me following him. Bobby started going faster and faster. I tried to keep up, but I wasn't sure if I could. Bobby's coaster was really speeding, and I was afraid he'd fly off the tracks. I was afraid I'd fly off the tracks too. And just as I was about to do that, I woke up.

I wish Carole were here so I could tell her about the dream. She's good at interpreting them. But she's about to fly off to Paris. I'm not going to bother her with crap from my psyche.

I wonder if the dream has anything to do with my seeing Bobby earlier today at Joe's. He was so frustrated, I felt bad for him. I hope he and his father make up. I don't have fights with Dad like he did—that's more Ray's job,

LOL. But it did make me think more about the pressure my folks put on me. I'm frustrated just like Bobby. Wanting to live my life in my own way is not selfish, is it? But what is my own way? Like I said to Bobby, I still don't know where I fit in, do I?

Good questions. Enough of those rattling around in my brain these days. Can't I focus on something fun for a change? Like what? Sitting there with Bobby in the park, overlooking Boston, our hands touching? Yeah, that was nice. Really nice. Why does the start of summer seem so long ago now?

*

Today I was in my favorite place again. Yeah, I guess I'm spending a lot of time on my rock in the woods lately. With everything going on, it's the only place I can think and figure things out. Not that I'm successful in getting answers. And the Big Guy's not talking. But at least this place calms me down.

Until today. Today, I was sitting there, thinking about everything and nothing, when I heard a noise. A voice, or was it two voices? Not too far away. I got really quiet and sat still, listening hard. I made out one voice. It was Ray's.

What was my brother doing here? I was about to go over when I made out another voice, and then two more, one of them a girl's. There was some laughter, and then they went quiet. I held my breath and didn't move a muscle. Whatever they were doing, I was sure they wanted privacy. And they wouldn't be happy if Ray's clod of a big brother came bouncing through the woods with a cheerful, "Hi, guys! What's up?"

And then I smelled the pot. The smell was unmistakable. I knew some guys at school who smoked it and we had lectures about it, once even by the cops. But my little brother?

I forgot all about Bobby, and started obsessing—yeah, that's the right word, obsessing about Ray. Even if he will be thirteen soon, he's still a kid for Chrissake! And already smoking pot? What about other drugs? I wish I could be a better older brother to him, but we're just so different. And he's so angry. I know Mom and Dad aren't perfect, but they're not that bad. I'd like to be able to talk to Ray, though it's getting harder and harder. Ever since he and Dad were called to school by Sister Hell Dog, the principal, because they thought he'd stolen something. He denied it, and they couldn't prove anything, so he got off easy. And luckily Dad didn't punish him badly the way he often does.

But still he's angry. I wish I could help him. But how? I can't change him or stop his fights with Dad. Still, I'm Ray's big brother. I should be there for him. And I feel bad.

Anyway, I sat on that rock, hardly breathing, for what seemed like hours. At one point someone started walking closer. It was a guy who shouted something back to his friends, and then stopped. I was terrified he saw me, but he was just taking a leak. I heard more laughter when he rejoined the group. I could make out Ray's voice as they shared some jokes. Ray laughed too. I realized I never hear him laugh at home, so it was good to hear him sounding happy for once, even if it was here.

Finally, after some more jokes I heard them leave slowly. I stayed on that rock longer, not wanting to run into them on my way home.

Now that I am home, I'm thinking about Ray again. Should I say something to him? Or keep quiet? But what would I say? "I heard you guys out in the woods. And I know what you were smoking. Be careful." That's so lame. What if I added something about Dad? Trying to scare Ray. Tell him what Dad would do if he found out. That's worse than lame. First of all, Ray doesn't scare easily. And in second place, I would be a real asshole for doing it.

Man, why do things happen the way they do? I go to my spot in the woods to relax and this happens. No fair.

Okay, Big Guy, what are you trying to tell me this time? Does this mean you are finally talking to me, ha ha? Too bad because it's not the way I was hoping for.

*

Okay, okay. Does the Big Guy—*if* He exists—really have it in for gay people? I keep telling myself that's not true, but today at church I started wondering all over again.

Mom has started insisting we go to Lith mass every Sunday again. We used to go, off and on, but then we stopped. It was a long drive to Southie in Boston, and Dad said we can worship God in any language. Besides, there aren't many Liths left in South Boston. The immigrants from the Old Country settled there in the old days, but then they moved up in the world like we did and scattered to the suburbs. So the Lith mass is pretty empty. Kind of sad really, with only the last of the Lith holdouts—mostly older folks and just a few younger types who don't need canes or walkers.

Dad sees some of his drinking buddies during the brunch they have downstairs after Mass, so he doesn't really mind going. And Mom sometimes sings in the choir so that's why she likes it. And she's decided to join the board of the Lith Nerds—I mean, the Futurists—this fall. I don't know what's gotten into her lately, but she's becoming a real activist, schmoozing and glad-handing everyone at brunch like a real Washington pol. Even more than Dad, who does his share of glad-handing too. Why are they both about to take the US citizenship test if they're still so big on being in Lith life?

Anyway, like Dad, I don't think God cares how we worship Him. But sometimes I swear He likes to keep after me, show me He's still around, even if I think I don't believe in Him at times.

Today's mass was celebrated by this cranky old priest, who seems to have a chip on his shoulder about anything fun. And wouldn't you know it, today his sermon was on families and sex. He talked about how families were important and said it was our responsibility to stop them from falling apart. Yeah, okay, nothing wrong with that. Then he began talking about sex and sin, and all the people who were sinning every day, especially with sex. He mentioned gays too. I don't know if it was my imagination, but I thought he was looking right at me when he talked about gays. Said it was our responsibility to stop all immoral behavior.

I wanted to sink through the floor and hide, but instead I tried to pretend nothing was going on. I glanced over at Mom and Dad and Ray, but they didn't seem bothered by what he was saying. Didn't even seem to be listening that carefully. I suddenly wanted to scream and yell out, "Wait! I'm here and I'm not immoral. I don't want to be sinning. I want to be a good guy. I am a good guy!"

I left Mass in a cold sweat. And I started getting depressed. Usually at brunch I can at least enjoy some food while Mom is schmoozing and glad-handing with everybody. But not today. I barely ate anything. I just sat there thinking about everything the priest said and got even more depressed. Dad even asked me if I was okay, and I had to pretend real hard that I was fine.

Ray was in a good mood for a change on the ride home and tried to joke with me, making fun of the old priest. But I was the silent one this time. I tried to tell myself to get over it, that there are a lot of ignorant people in the world, and priests are people too. And the ignorant ones are not talking for God. That so many things I had been told growing up might not be true after all. I wish I could really believe it. Because it all still gets overwhelming to think about sometimes.

*

The Fourth of July. A time for picnics, ice cream, fireworks, and fun, celebrating the birthday of this country. Right? Wrong, not in our family, especially not this year.

It's the other time besides Thanksgiving we usually get together with Mom's relatives the Shalinskai (pronounced Sh-ahh-linss-kai), or as I call them, the S-heads, ha ha. They haven't gotten less snooty since we saw them last year. Mr. S-head just got appointed head surgeon at one of the local hospitals. Mrs. S-head is still blonde, elegant, and very active in Lith immigrant affairs. Jonas is now seventeen and will be starting his senior year in high school and already knows he's going to Harvard to be a surgeon like his daddy. And thirteen-year-old Jolanda knows she's even more beautiful and is already trying out for some modeling gigs.

Since the S-heads come to our house for Thanksgiving, we go to their house for the Fourth of July picnic. Their house is a huge McMansion in Wellesley, one of those fancy suburbs where the humongous houses are hidden behind high shrubs. They have a huge yard, too, with some woods in back, where they set up chairs and picnic tables. The food is catered. Some food is American with little Stars and Stripes pinned into the hamburgers and hot dogs. And some food is Lithuanian, with yellow-green-red Lithuanian flags pinned into the meat pies and scary-looking cheeses. "We're good, proud Lithuanians and good, proud Americans," the S-heads proclaim all the time. I can vouch for the fact they're proud. Whether they're good is another story.

The only thing that saves this party is the S-heads invite other friends and neighbors too. So I can usually get lost in the crowd or take a quiet walk in the woods where no one will miss me until it's time to go home. But not this year. I tried to become inconspicuous again, but when I tried to grab one of those patriotic hot dogs I found myself cornered by Mrs. S-head.

She asked me what I was doing this summer, and I told her about working at Ed's Garage. That didn't impress her. She asked me if I was going to camp or taking part in any other Lith activities. She's head of all sorts of immigrant Lith organizations and is glad Mom plans to run for the board of the Futurists organization. And of course she presses Mom about her kids. I know she gives Mom an earful whenever she can.

Of course I got one today too. *"Kas su tavim yra, Arvydai?"* *"Tau patiks stovykla, Arvydai."* *"Susitiksi gražių lietuvaičių, Arvydai."* *"Neužmiršk savo paveldo, Arvydai."*

"What's wrong with you, RV?" "You'll like camp, RV." "You'll meet pretty Lithuanian girls, RV." "Don't forsake your heritage, RV."

There's that word again, heritage. And wouldn't you know it, Dad showed up at that moment. All I could do was stare and shrug my shoulders as Dad added his two cents while Mrs. S-head continued to tut-tut, the way she does, her steel-blonde hair catching the glints of the sun as she shook her head back and forth, giving her an extra dose of authority.

I thought they were finished and was about to escape when who shows up but Cousin Jonas. Of course he's going to camp, and even acting as a counselor, proving his Super-Lith credentials. He loved it when Dad praised him and his mother stood beside him, showering her love on him.

Then he turned to me. "Come on, RV. Why don't you come? We'll have fun!"

Yeah sure. Like the last time he told me we'd have fun at that Lith function we went to. When he convinced me to smoke and drink with his buddies and caused me to throw up in front of everybody.

It took all my energy not to give in. I said I'd think about it, which is my usual way of getting people off my back. Why couldn't I just say, "No, thanks. I really need a break from Lith life. I'm already giving up time by working at Ed's Garage. And I want to spend time with Bobby, and I want to get to know him better."

Why is that so hard? Or am I just a wimp?

Finally, Mrs. S-head was done tut-tutting, and Dad and Jonas started talking about something else. I made an excuse about wanting something to drink and walked away. I grabbed a Coke and made my way to the woods.

I actually love it there, even though it's so close to the S-heads' house. It's quiet and cool, and a burbling stream shuts out most of the noise of the party. So I can walk on the little path there or sit by the stream and just chill.

Why are they always after me to do Lith things? Why is it so important for them? Why can't I live my life the way I want?

I don't want to live their lives. I want to live my life!

Oh, oh. I'm starting to sound like Bobby. What does that mean?

*

Well, I had one victory at least. I was so upset after yesterday's party, it gave me the energy to confront Mom and Dad when they asked me about camp again. I wore them down and got out of going. They finally agreed not to force me to go. Maybe they're just too busy with their citizenship stuff to have much energy left for me. Good. A little crap off my shoulders at least. No need to worry about being the camp nerd or putting up with Jonas or making a fool of myself with a baseball bat or a football. Or any kind of ball!

Wait! Stop it, RV! Don't get too excited and jinx yourself. You know things can change quickly. You've seen it happen before. Mom and Dad just might turn around and get you involved in something else. Something worse. So keep your head down and watch yourself. It's the best way of keeping summer for yourself. At least the parts of it you haven't given away yet.

Chapter Four

Citizenship

Mom and Dad had a bad argument. Okay, so what else is new? I should be used to them. But I'm not. I'll never get used to them. Especially when those big dark eyes of Dad's get bigger and darker and you know he's ready to blow his stack. Then you better leave him alone because the smallest thing will set him off.

That's what happened today. Dad came back from work in a bad mood already. He had an argument with a coworker on the construction site, who ended up saying something about immigrants and telling him to go back to the Old Country. They almost got into a fistfight. Dad even has to go to the head office later this week to see the HR people.

Then, at dinner Mom reminded him their appointment in the citizenship process was coming up. Dad told her he was in no mood to think about citizenship. That got Mom upset. She asked him if he was backing out again. He told her not to lecture him. She told him she was going forward with him or without him. More angry words went back and forth. Then fists on the table and doors slamming. Mom left the kitchen and Dad started staring at me, as if I was part of the argument too. I knew it was time for me to leave also.

If becoming a citizen is supposed to be good, why is it causing so much extra fighting, at least in my family? I think it's the crazy process of getting there. At least that's part of it. Getting your green card is only the first step, and that can take forever. After that, there's more paperwork and more steps. And everything costs money.

Since Dad didn't want to spend money and hire a lawyer at first, he and Mom tried to do everything themselves. Correction. They made me help them, since I'm supposedly the smart one in English. Filing out the N-400 form, the official request for citizenship, was so much fun. It runs about twenty pages and there were questions like "how many hours have you been out of the country in the last five years?" and "what's your relationship to your children?" Duh. I wanted to put down "stressful." Too bad that wasn't one of the choices.

The form I helped fill out came back months later because the immigration people said there were mistakes. So there was another fight. Mom won that one, getting Dad to hire a lawyer, though he had to spend almost two thousand more dollars. That form went through okay, and they finally got a letter telling them to come in for the screening and background check, where they will get fingerprinted, photographed, and stuff like that. That's what they have to do next, and of course it will cost more money.

No wonder Dad's procrastinating. Makes me want to procrastinate, too, especially since Dad has said I'll have to help him prepare for the step after that: the test and interview. (Pro-cras-ti-nate. My new ten-cent word. Sounds kind of dirty, doesn't it? Procrastinate. Something people do in the dark.)

Do I really want to be like Dad? No. I don't really want to procrastinate my life. But then I can't really blame him for being angry at someone calling him names just because he has an accent. Or having to prove he's good enough to live in this country, when he works just as hard or harder than anyone.

But I can't blame Mom for getting exasperated with him, either. She just wants to go through the process and get on with her life. Her new life. She says she's ready for it. And she seems to be.

Today I walked in on her in the kitchen. She was on the phone, talking to a friend from work. From what I could gather, they were planning to start a jewelry business together.

Man, Mom is something else! Just earlier this year, she lost money and some jewelry in that consignment store deal when the guy she'd gone into business with closed up shop and ran off with everything. Sure, she cried for what, one day? But look at her now. Laughing and making plans for another store.

Dad gave her a hard time about it, saying he wasn't going to let her touch any more of the family savings, but she told him she didn't need it. She said her friend would put up the front money and Mom would pay her back slowly as they made money.

Dad asked what if they didn't make money.

But Mom shook her head and told him he was being negative. She told him the way to make it in this country is to be positive. So she was being positive. Dad gave her a dirty look but didn't say anything.

And when I saw her today, talking into the phone resting on her shoulder while she jotted down numbers on a pad of paper, she already looked like the busy businesswoman. She was being positive all right. And she certainly did look ready to become an American citizen.

Mom and Dad make me wonder if I'm more positive or more negative. One thing's for sure. I should just be glad I was born here. I don't have to go through the process of becoming a citizen or prove anything. One less thing to worry and be negative about. There's enough of that ten times over.

*

Something bad must be afoot, as they say in the old books. I did my shift at Ed's Garage today, and it started out pretty well. No, very well. Mean Melissa wasn't there. It was me and Ed cleaning up the place, throwing out a little more junk, and pumping gas. Ed even let me pump a couple of times. And I did great, if I say so myself.

Ed seemed in his usual good mood, trading bad jokes with the customers and laughing most of the time. At one point he went back into the store and asked me to take care of the next few customers. Then a car pulled up with a couple of young guys in it. They were playing loud music and talking and laughing loudly in a language I couldn't understand. They teased me, too, making jokes about the way I looked and telling me to bring them drinks from the store.

Then a couple of them got out of the car and went into the store. While they shopped, I finished pumping the gas and told the driver how much it was. He started fishing for his wallet, but was taking a long time getting his money out. The next thing I knew, the guys ran out of the store with bags of candy and chips and drinks. Ed started running after them, yelling for them to pay.

But by the time he got outside, the guys had already jumped into the car. The driver gunned the engine, and they sped off.

"Get the license plate number! Get the license plate number!" Ed was yelling to me.

I tried to read it as they were speeding off, but the back license plate had been covered up with a piece of paper so I couldn't see anything. All I could see was that one of them stuck his hand out of the window and gave us the finger. And they turned the music back on real loud.

Ed ran up to me and put his hand on my shoulder to steady himself. He was panting a lot, as if he'd just run a mile. "Did you get the license plate number?" he asked between breaths.

I shook my head. "No. It was covered up."

"What make of car was it?"

"I'm sorry, I didn't notice that either." At that point I wished I listened to Dad more when he made me help him fix the car or wash it. Yeah, Dad loves everything about his car. I just wish he didn't try to force me to like it too. "The car was black and old," I said kind of meekly. "And seemed a little beat up."

Ed was still panting. He looked angry. I knew my description was pretty lame.

"I just remembered there was a dent on the driver's side door. And a big scratch."

If that helped, Ed was ignoring it. He looked angrier and angrier. He swore. "Those fucking spics! I'm going to call the cops. Those spics aren't getting away."

"I don't think they were talking Spanish," I said before I could stop myself.

"What makes you so sure?" Ed asked angrily. "Are you some kind of expert?"

I shook my head, trying to stay calm. "No. I, uh, take Spanish in school and I know a little bit."

"A little bit! And so you were able to tell in those few seconds that it wasn't Spanish!"

I nodded.

"I'm still calling the cops. Those spics, or whatever they were, are not going to get away. It's the second time this has happened in as many months, and I'm not going to be taken for a chump anymore! You hear me, RV? No more foreign assholes will take advantage of jolly old Ed!"

With that he started making his way back toward the store.

The rest of the day was painful. Gone was Ed the jokester. In his place was someone totally different. Someone very angry. It seems like anger is all around me these days.

I was nervous all day. I had seen how Melissa had gotten angry when I knocked over that shelf. Ed already didn't seem thrilled with me for what I said about the guys not talking Spanish. What else would make him angry?

I tried to listen when he called the police. But he gave me a dirty look and lowered his voice. I had to leave the store because another customer pulled up. Ed talked to the police for a while, his voice rising sometimes, and he kept motioning with his hands.

If he got ripped off like that before, I could see why he would be upset. I guess I would be, too, if it was my store. But what about the whole business thinking they were Hispanic? Would I assume that's what those guys were, even if I wasn't sure?

*

Another typical dinner at our house, today. I was silent, thinking about what happened at Ed's Garage. Mom and Dad weren't talking much either, probably lost in whatever things they were thinking about. The only one talking was Ray. He was chattering away about a movie he had seen, even complimented Mom on the food. The fact no one paid much attention to what he was saying didn't seem to bother him.

At the end of dinner Mom made a point of saying she was going to do some studying for the citizenship test. She glanced at Dad but he ignored her. She ignored him back and got up and left the room. Dad left, too, without saying a word. So that was it. The citizenship was on their minds, just in different ways. Getting citizenship is supposed to be something good, right? So, as I keep asking myself, why does it cause people so much stress?

"Great dinner. Great conversation. Great family," Ray mumbled sarcastically.

I was about to say something rude to him, but decided to keep my mouth shut. Didn't want to add yet another fight into the family dynamics. They're bad enough as it is.

Before going upstairs to my room, I passed by the little study room where Dad keeps his papers. He was sitting in a chair reading a letter. From the crumpled looks of it, I'm pretty sure I know what the letter was. One of the letters his father wrote to Dad when he was in prison. Back in the Old Country. Dad's father was an activist, protesting the Russian occupation of the country, and he was thrown into prison for a year. He wrote Dad a lot of letters. I sometimes see the pile on Dad's desk when I pass his study. Dad sits in his chair reading them. Or sometimes he's just sitting in the chair, staring out into space, holding one of the letters in his lap.

One day, Dad read me one of the letters from his father. He was writing about his daily life in prison. Said it was hard, but that he was doing okay. Told Dad to keep the faith, that he would be home soon. And then Dad got to a part that choked him up. I could tell because Dad read it in fits and starts, very slowly, as if he wasn't sure he could continue. His father apologized for bringing hardship to his family, and he asked Dad to understand. Asked Dad to take care of his sisters and their mother until he got home. Said some things were worth hardship if you really believed in the sanctity in what you were fighting for. Don't know why he used the word sanctity, but he did. Wonder if Dad felt something religious about it.

The sad thing is, Granddad never got out of prison. Something happened and he died before he could get out. The authorities said it was an accident. No one believed that, but no one could do anything about it either.

Sometimes, when I see Dad sitting there, holding one of the letters in his lap, I want to go comfort him. And learn more about Granddad. And what's in more of the other letters. But Dad doesn't look like he wants to be comforted. Or talk. He looks like he wants to be left alone.

So I stop myself. I tell myself the letters must be very private or Dad would talk about them. And I hope maybe someday Dad will tell me more.

But I can't help wondering how much the letters have to do with Dad hesitating about getting his citizenship. He's also got a brother back in the Old Country, an uncle I've never met. Uncle Vlad. Dad and Uncle Vlad don't talk or email much. Dad says he's gone over to the other side, whatever the other side is. Too bad. Dad is the only one of his family here in the US, and he doesn't communicate with his only brother who's six thousand miles away. Makes me sad. I think about Ray and me. We don't talk much now either. But if we are the same way throughout our lives, that will really make me depressed.

Becoming a citizen of a new country means you forget the past and move forward, doesn't it? So to Dad it must mean forgetting the family he comes from. Including his three sisters? He communicates with them all the time. I wonder what they talk about. Does Dad really want to go back to the Old Country the way he threatens sometimes?

Would I ever want to forget my family? Sometimes, sure. But deep down, would I really? No. It makes me sad to even think about that.

Chapter Five

Chickening Out

Finally saw Bobby again. I was so happy to see him. He'll be going to football camp soon, and I'll miss him. So I wanted to enjoy our time together as much as possible. It's so great when we're together. The world seems to disappear, and it's just me and him. Even if it's not in a special place like the park looking over Boston or the woods behind the ball field, being with him still feels great.

Today I went to his house. We were sitting there on the bed in his room, leaning against the wall, talking. Well, mostly. There was more complaining than talking. At least on Bobby's part. His parents were home, but Bobby didn't care. He locked the door to his room and started mouthing off about his father again. He was pissed off at him for making Bobby work for his friend.

"Joe Moocher. Joe A-hole is more like it," Bobby said. "Can't believe my father likes him. Mr. A-hole thinks he's so cool, but all he cares about is money. I could give a shit about his friggin' millions. He can shove them up where the sun don't shine, as far as I'm concerned."

At least he laughed when he said that. But it wasn't a happy laugh. More like the frustrated one he has whenever he talks about the job. He started telling me all sorts of crap about the guy, about his yelling at people over the phone, giving Bobby a hard time because he got the wrong file or something, and being rude and obnoxious to everybody he comes across.

I got a little tired of hearing about it and tried to get Bobby to talk about something else. I asked him about other things he was doing this summer, but that only got him complaining about his father again.

"I wish he didn't care so much about my success," Bobby said. "When I'm in school it's all about my grades and the teams I join. He so proud of me and talks me up to all his friends. Mom, too, but he does it more."

"But that's good, isn't it?"

"Yes and no. I want to do well and all that. But do I know what I want to do for a career? No. And there's something else. Something underneath all that pride my father supposedly has in me. Can't explain it. But it's scary. Makes me feel if I screw up on anything there'll be hell to pay."

Bobby picked up the pillow from behind his back and angrily threw it on the floor.

"Now it's all this summer stuff," he continued. "Making me work for his friend. Asking me what I'm learning. Expecting me to love it, of course. And even the football camp. I thought I wanted to go, but now I'm not so sure."

"I thought you were really looking forward to football camp," I said, surprised.

"Yeah, I am. But I wish I could forget all this other crap and just concentrate on the football. All this other stuff sucks."

He seemed almost as upset as the time he asked me to meet him at Joe's. I didn't know what to say. I just looked at him, feeling bad and useless, not knowing how to comfort him.

Then he said something a little strange. "Hope I'll do okay."

"What do you mean?"

"At football camp."

"Why wouldn't you do okay?"

"I need a lot of practice. And there are a lot of great players out there. I just hope I don't disappoint myself." Before I could say anything, he shook his head and let out another angry laugh. "There I go, putting pressure on myself. Like my father's pressure isn't enough."

"But—but everyone says you're so good."

"I could be better. Much better. I'm pretty good at catching the ball and running with it, but I don't have a great arm."

"A great arm?"

"Yeah, if I want to be a quarterback. A quarterback needs to throw like a rocket and hit his target."

"Oh. Is that the position you're trying out for?"

"This isn't really about trying out for a position but improving certain skills."

"Oh."

Bobby finally smiled a little. "RV, how much do you know about football?"

"Not much I guess."

"But it's the great American pastime. More than baseball."

"I didn't grow up thinking about American stuff. My family focused on other stuff."

"Other stuff like what?"

"Like I've told you. Communism. Capitalism. Terrorism. Socialism. Fun stuff like that."

Bobby laughed, picked up another pillow, and threw it at me. "You poor guy. Don't you want to learn American stuff?"

"Sure."

"Good. I'll teach you."

I shrugged. "I don't know. You tried to teach me how to shoot baskets and look how that turned out."

Bobby smiled. "Well, maybe football will be different. Hey," he added, getting excited. "First lesson. I'll have to take you to a Patriots game. Would you want to do that?"

"Yeah, sure."

"And then I'll take you out to the field and throw some footballs at you. You can practice catching, and I'll practice throwing."

"Ah, okay." I was glad to see Bobby looking happier, though I didn't really know how I felt. Watching a football game with Bobby is fine. But practicing it? I cringed, not wanting to remember how bad I was at shooting hoops with him.

Bobby laughed, as if reading my thoughts again. "Don't worry, RV, I'll go easy on you."

The next thing I knew Bobby had jumped on me and pinned me to the bed. "There. This is your first tackle. That's not so bad, is it?"

"Yeah, right. How often do you play football on a bed?"

"Not often enough," Bobby said, laughing again. Then he leaned closer to me and whispered, "C'mon, RV, do you want to try another game?"

"Another game?"

"Yeah. Do you want to do the Big M together?"

We talked about the Big M once, masturbation. We admitted to each other that we did it. And we liked it. But masturbating together? I was embarrassed just thinking about it.

"But your parents—"

"Don't worry, the door is locked."

Bobby's hands went to the zipper on his pants, but I told him to stop, surprised at my own boldness.

"Don't be scared," Bobby said.

"I'm not," I lied. "I'm just—I'm just not ready."

I don't know what that was supposed to mean, but I said it. I guess I was buying time because I was scared, and I didn't want Bobby to see.

"C'mon, RV," Bobby said. "Some of the guys on the football team do it."

"How do you know?"

"I hear guys talk about it."

"You do?"

"Yeah."

"And they do it with each other?"

"A couple of them, yeah."

"Isn't that, well, like a gay thing?"

"I don't think so. They talk about girls all the time." He gave me a funny look, like the one Carole gives me sometimes. "So, how about it, RV? Do you want to try it with me?" My face must have shown a lot of other things because then Bobby said, "RV, are you really that innocent? It's not a big deal."

I blushed. A lot. For the first time in my life Bobby was making me feel bad. And because it was Bobby, I felt terrible. I didn't want him to see it, but I couldn't help myself. Will I ever learn not to blush?

Bobby is still Bobby, though. When he noticed how I was feeling, he let up on me. "Okay, RV. If you're not into it, you're not into it. I thought you might be." He got up off the bed and went to pick up the pillows he had thrown on the floor. "I was just curious and thought you might be too."

He put the pillows back on the bed, but didn't lie down next to me, sitting up instead. We kept quiet. I could tell Bobby was disappointed, and I wondered what else he was thinking.

Luckily, I didn't have much time to dwell on it. Bobby's father started calling him, wanting something. So Bobby unlocked the door, and we both went downstairs. I made up some excuse that I had to do something at home and left.

*

I'm still wondering why I chickened out with Bobby. Yeah, it's really bothering me, and I can't sleep. So here I am trying to figure it out.

Why did I say no to him? Was I just scared or did I not really want to do it? How can one tell the difference? Does it mean it's sex if you do the Big M with someone?

Bobby called me innocent, and it wasn't a compliment, not by a long shot. That really hurts. So what am I going to do about it? Just say yes the next time he asks me? After all, he said it wasn't a big deal. Why did it feel like a big deal to me? I feel stupid. Did I screw things up with Bobby? What if there's no next time?

And what about the gay stuff? I thought Bobby worried about it even more than I did. But he didn't seem to, not in this case. Maybe football jocks don't worry about doing the Big M together if they're talking about their girlfriends while they do it.

I should have asked Bobby if he talked about Cynthia Hoevermeyer, but I don't want to know. How would he feel if I started bragging about Carole? Like that guy in math class, Silver, who brags about all the stuff he does with his girlfriend.

Yeah, RV, as if you could get away with it. Don't even go there! People would probably see through you pretty quickly. People like Duffy and Doyle. And you don't want to think about the things they might do to you in the locker room.

Stop it, RV! Go to bed and forget everything. You don't have answers to any of these questions, and the Big Guy is not cooperating and giving you any clues. So you just have to stop trying to figure things out or you'll wear out your brain.

Chapter Six

Two Nice Things and a Picnic

Two nice things happened today that distracted me from thinking about Bobby for the time being. First I got a WhatsApp text from Carole. It was in French, of course.

Bonjour, RV! Comment allez-vous? Paris est très belle! J'aime beaucoup Paris!

I'm taking Spanish at school, but I know a little French, too, since I'm such a language nut. So Carole's texts weren't hard to translate.

Hi, RV. How are you? Paris is beautiful. I like Paris a lot!

It would have been fun to answer her in French, but apart from *bonjour* and *au revoir* I can't write in French. So I answered her in Spanish, LOL.

Hola, qué bueno saber de ti, Carole! ¿Cómo son los croissants? Todo bien aquí.

Good ol' Carole. Don't know if she understood everything, but she answered back in French and continued in Spanish. Pretty cool, huh? A conversation in French and Spanish. Oh, I miss Carole! From what I understood, she told me she and her father were in a nice apartment near the Arch of Triumph and she was enjoying exploring the neighborhood. She especially enjoyed going to the little shop, the *tabac,* around the corner where the little old man who ran it was friendly and helped her with her French.

I'm glad she sounds so happy. Having her in Paris is still not as good as having her here in Boston with me, but WhatsApp is a close second, I guess. It will be good to hear about her adventures. Maybe I'll get to Paris someday too. Would love to see the whole world, though I have to figure out my own world first.

But, as I said, I got two nice surprises today. The other one was a text from Mr. Aniso, saying hello and asking how I'm enjoying my summer. I haven't seen Mr. Aniso since the last day of school, when he came back to the graduation ceremonies and we gave him that standing ovation. I was glad he said he's doing well, gaining strength, and even exercising a little. He told me he'll definitely be back teaching this fall. And he even gave me his cell number. "So you can text me anytime you want to talk or just say hi," he said.

I texted him back right away. I told him I was glad to hear from him and thanked him for his number. Told him what was going on with me—not much really, hearing from Carole, and about working in Ed's Garage. Told him Bobby and I didn't see as much of each other as we wanted, since we were both so busy. Really wanted to tell him more, but that promise to Bobby keeps getting in the way.

Sometimes I get mad at Bobby for making me promise not to tell anyone he might be gay. And I get mad at myself for sticking to that promise. What if I did break it? Especially to someone like Mr. Aniso. What would be the harm?

But, of course, I didn't go there. Breaking my promise to Bobby would feel like a betrayal of him. And that's the last thing I want to do. Wouldn't want anyone to do it to me, either, would I?

So I just told Mr. Aniso a few more things I'd been doing and stopped after that. It's okay, I told myself. I was just happy to have this text exchange with him. He's my favorite teacher, even though I like other ones too. But he's special, at least to me. And it makes me feel kind of honored that he wrote me, as dramatic as it sounds. But it's true. Makes me feel so much less alone.

*

A summer picnic in the country. Sounds so nice and relaxing, doesn't it? A way for immigrants to be with each other so they feel less alone and can celebrate their heritage. Ah, yes, our all-important heritage.

That's what it's about at the annual Lithuanian Family Day Picnic. It takes place at the Most Holy Spiritual Renewal Center. It's a convent. A real convent with real nuns. That's where we were today.

Have to admit I used to like the picnic as a kid. The convent is in a pretty location in the countryside, surrounded by fields and hills in Nowheresville, Connecticut. Those days the family would come and spend the day breathing fresh, unpolluted air, having picnics on the grass, eating all sorts of crazy Lith foods, and socializing with friends. I did too.

These days some things are still the same. The air is still unpolluted (I think), the foods are still crazy, and my parents and Ray still see their friends.

But for me today was different. I didn't see too many people my age. Not sure why. Are my friends not coming now they're in high school? Do they have new friends?

Like a lot of things these days, that makes me sad too. We used to have fun, catching up with each other, hanging out, and making fun of the adults who were eating and drinking too much. Things have changed. Another sign that life is more complicated than you thought when you were a kid.

I was still trying to have a good time, I really was. Even at Mass, which is the first thing one does at these picnics. Hey, what do you expect from a picnic given by nuns? I came to terms with that ages ago. At any mass I used to get the hour to pass by without too much pain by making up my own stories about all the characters in the Bible.

Like my stories about Adam and Eve. In one of them I had them arguing with God when he threw them out of the Garden of Eden, telling Him why they deserved a second chance. In another one I had them arguing with each other over who was more to blame for their eating that stupid apple.

The church at the convent is pretty, mostly white, with stained glass windows and modern art in front. The art here in this church is too modern to inspire me with stories. Instead I found myself actually listening to the sermon. I was afraid the priest would talk about sex again, as many of them do. But this priest talked about Christ's message of forgiveness and who it's aimed at. He said everybody. Got me wondering. Is it designed for people like me? People who are still trying to figure out who they are? Or aren't?

Then I did start making up a story. Imagined me coming up to Christ and telling him about Bobby. And Carole. And even doing the Big M. What would He say about all that? Could I even talk to him about being gay? That scared me and got me excited at the same time. Talking with Christ about being gay. What a concept. Would He want to do that? For the first time in my life, I was almost sorry when Mass ended because I wanted to think about that a little more.

After Mass it's always time for lunch. From the spiritual to the pigging out stage. And Mom and Dad really do pig out at these picnics, stuffing themselves silly. I know for them it's comfort food. More like discomfort, if you ask me. Discomfort for the rest of us. Dad can't get enough cabbage. *Kopūstai. Kopūstai. Kopūstai.* That's all he talks about all weekend: cabbage soup, sausage with cabbage, boiled cabbage, cabbage, cabbage, cabbage. Good for him and bad for us because it gives him gas, gas, and more gas. Why do I come from a culture that's so big on gassy foods?

Mom doesn't go for the cabbage, thank God, or else we'd really be in trouble. She's the potato queen. Loves *kugelis*. A cake made from potatoes. Really? Mom says it's delicious, especially with *rūgštus pienas*. I don't even know how to describe that. It's fermented milk or some concoction like that.

At least they also have hot dogs and hamburgers, for us uninitiated types not into the glories of Lith cuisine. Mom and Dad say Ray and I don't know what we're missing by going for the all-American stuff. I know what we're missing: cholesterol. Did I forget to mention that Dad's *kopūstai come* with bacon bits? And Mom's *kugelis* does too. Plus a big dose of sour cream on top. And they say hot dogs and hamburgers aren't healthy.

It's usually around this time I try to escape these culinary delights, like Ray does, and hang out with a friend or two. Like I said, I used to be able to find some friends at these events to hang out with. When I used to go to Lith school on Saturdays, it was a great way to see friends in summer when there was no school. Not this year. Didn't see anyone after having my hot dogs, so I snuck away, found myself a nice vantage point that looks over fields and woods in the distance, and started reading.

Being alone in nature makes me feel good. The nice surroundings at this convent make it especially good. Everything is green around here, at least in summer when we come: huge leafy trees, big fields with tall grass, and more fields in the distance. And it's so peaceful, except for the sounds of nature you hear off and on. Nature's been here a long time and will be here for a long time after we're gone. Makes one think, in a good way, how little our troubles matter.

I read for a while and then remembered it was time for the Lith folk dances. I have to admit that's something I like about this culture. To me it's another sign that it's not all bad. Mom and Dad enrolled me in a folk dance group when I was a kid, which was fun. The dances are kind of like American square dances but Lith-style: accordion music, twirling with your partner, doing fancy moves and complicated footsteps. I got pretty good at it and enjoyed practicing and even wearing those poofy national costumes when we performed in public. What can I say? It took more time out of my life, but I made friends. So I can't say all Lith stuff is bad, can I?

The dances were performed on a big lawn by kids from the camp Mom and Dad were going to send me to. I have to admit something else. Watching them twirling and doing those fancy moves made me feel a little nostalgic. Why did I say no to camp? Camp is not all bad, either. If Bobby is going to a camp, maybe I can go to one too.

I kept thinking about that while watching the dances. When they were finished, someone tapped me on the shoulder.

"Hey, RV."

I turned around. It was Al, one of my old Saturday school friends. He was one of the dancers and was sweaty and out of breath, since he had just finished dancing.

"Hey, RV," he said again.

"Hey, Al. Good to see you."

"You too. What's up?"

"Not much. What's up with you, Al?"

"It's Algis. Remember?"

Oh, yeah. Algis now wanted to be called by his full Lith name. He's become one of those Super Liths, into his family roots and his heritage. Says Algis is his "real" name. Dad loves him.

Okay. People deserve to be called how they want to be called. I tried again. "So, Algis. What have you been up to?"

"We're missing you at camp."

"Oh, yeah? It's going well?"

"Yeah. The food's better this year."

"That's good."

"And I'm in a pretty good cabin. Met some cool New York kids."

"Oh, yeah?"

"Yeah."

My running joke with Al—can't think of him by any other name. Not the Al who was my friend, anyway. When he and I were at camp together we used to hang out with some kids from New York. Of course they thought they were cooler than the Boston kids. We did learn cool stuff from them, including about things we weren't supposed to know, ha ha. If Dad only knew about that part!

Al and I talked for a minute or two longer, but then we ran out of things to say to each other. We just stood there for a minute or two, awkwardly nodding and saying "Yeah." "Sure." "Good to see you." "Keep in touch" and stuff like that. After a minute or two more, Al left, saying he had to change from his dancing costume.

It's strange. We used to be pretty good friends, hanging out at Lith school and these other events. But now I didn't know what to say to him. And I guess he didn't know what to say to me.

I started feeling bad again on the way home. Mom and Dad seemed happy, having stuffed themselves with all that cholesterol-packed food and partying with friends. They really feel at home at these events, don't they? No arguments or signs of stress today. No talk of citizenship or the jewelry business. Dad even gave Mom a hug and she hugged him back. They actually seemed happy with each other. Something I haven't seen in quite a while. So is that why their heritage is important to them? It keeps them close. And happy?

But what about my heritage? What does it do for me? I don't feel at home here anymore, like I used to. What does it say about me? Or these events?

Spent time thinking about Al too. Yeah I miss him, at least the Al before he became Algis. He was a good guy, and we used to have fun together. But now he's become Super Lith. And I've become what? Just someone with a bunch of questions.

Oh well. Told myself to stop worrying about the past and concentrate on the future. But what's that future going to be? Easy to ask but not easy to figure out.

Chapter Seven

Advice from Mr. Aniso

Was hoping to see Bobby today before he leaves for football camp tomorrow, but it didn't work out. He cancelled. Said his father wanted some help around the house, and he couldn't get away. Hope that's the real reason and not something else.

I've got to stop it imagining all of sorts of terrible things. It's just the way the summer's been going. Bobby will be gone for nearly three weeks. Makes me sad. No, sadder. It's not like I've seen him half as much as I'd like. Between his job and my job, and now football camp, there never seems to be enough time. Crazy, isn't it? So much for the lazy, languid days of summer.

Was hoping to take Bobby to my favorite spot in the woods, but I went there by myself today. Sitting on our rock and looking out at the hills in the distance did make me feel better, the way it always does. Like there's a future out there for me. And not just for me. For Bobby too. Maybe me and Bobby. And Carol. And everybody else.

But then, like sometimes happens, the sadness came back and the good feelings disappeared. The future wasn't something promising anymore, but there was that big fat question mark instead. I started thinking about chickening out with Bobby when he suggested the Big M and how he called me innocent. Still feel bad about that.

So was he really saying I'm too innocent to be with him? That he's actually one of the cool guys, something I'll never be?

I was about to leave when I heard a noise. Yup, it was my brother Ray's voice. But instead of a lot of other voices I just heard one other, a girl's. Well, well, my brother was with a girl. What were they doing? I could tell by the way they were talking quietly and giggling they were having a good time.

I didn't move, wanting and not wanting to hear them. And then I smelled the familiar odor of pot. It reminded me I had never talked to Ray about that first time when I overheard him with his friends and smelled the pot. So it wasn't just a one-time thing. I've been meaning to talk to Ray, but haven't yet. Did it just slip my mind? Ha! Be honest, RV. You chickened out. You didn't really want to talk to him about it because you didn't know what to say. That list of things you're chickening out on is growing longer.

Ray and the girl started giggling more loudly. And then whispering, saying things I couldn't hear. The pot smell became stronger. It made me mad. This was my spot, even if I wasn't sure it would always be good anymore. Couldn't Ray find another place for himself? And this pot business was serious for someone his age. For a second I had the crazy notion of bursting in on them and saying... What would I say? Give them a lecture? About what? Maybe Bobby was right. I was too innocent to lecture Ray about anything.

Luckily, I didn't go through with that idea. Instead I sat there on the rock frozen, thinking about Bobby and Carol and my brother. It took forever, but finally Ray and the girl left. I left, too, feeling sadder, not better. So much for a relaxing time in my favorite spot.

*

I sent Mr. Aniso a text. And he answered! I was a little nervous about it at first, started and stopped writing it a couple of times. But I just needed to talk to someone. Not only about the things I was chickening out on, but other stuff. Not sure what exactly, but stuff. About feeling sad and all the questions I have about myself. Carole's in Paris, and Bobby's at football camp. So Mr. Aniso is the only one left I trust.

I was scared at first. I mean, Mr. Aniso is an adult and I'm fifteen, so why would he want to get together with me? But I reread his first message to me, and he did say if I ever wanted to talk to him about anything I should feel free to contact him. Well, talking to him meant getting together with him, right? And there were a lot of things I wanted his advice on. So finally I did text, saying hello, asking him how he was feeling, and telling him if he did have some free time there were a few things I wanted to talk to him about.

He texted me back right away and said he'd be happy to get together with me. Whew! We settled on getting a slice at Joe's together. Wow. First Carole, then Bobby, and now Mr. Aniso. I was bringing all my close friends to Joe's. Maybe Joe should start paying me a referral fee.

I got there first because I was feeling nervous. Could I call Mr. Aniso a friend? Sure, I had told him some things about myself and about maybe being gay, but he was still a teacher. What did he really think of me? He'd been so supportive when I saw him in the hospital, but this was different. This was like trying to be equals. And were we? Could we ever be?

And what about me? Did I care that people might see me with him? Sure, this was an out-of-the-way place, but you never knew who could walk in. And nothing travels faster than rumors at school.

I kept thinking about these things when there he was, coming up to my booth. He was still using a cane but walking more steadily than at the graduating ceremony.

"Hey, RV. Good to see you," he said, a big smile lighting up his face. His smile made me feel a little better.

"Yeah, good to see you, too, Mr. Aniso," I said.

"So, this is Joe's Pizza." Mr. Aniso looked around and nodded. "Smells good. So what kind of pizza do you recommend I get?" he asked, sitting down. "I'm hungry."

I told him about some of the combinations I liked. He laughed. "Super jalapeño, huh? I better stay away from that! Don't want heartburn on top of everything else."

I decided I'd get a plain slice cheese slice. Still feeling a little nervous, I didn't want anything too complicated to upset my stomach, either. Mr. Aniso's choice was pepperoni.

"My treat," he said, getting up and going to the counter. He ordered the pizza slices and came back after a few minutes with both slices and a couple of Cokes.

"No strange meat or vegetables on my pizza," he said, laughing again. "Call me old-fashioned, but if you're going to go for pizza, pepperoni is the way to go."

I laughed too. "I like pepperoni too," I said. "But sometimes it's good to eat healthy. Or pretend to. And some people actually like the vegetables. Bobby Marshall, for instance. He loves green stuff on his pizza."

Mr. Aniso made a face. "Yechh, not me. I'm not ruining my pizza with vegetables." Then he turned serious. "So how is your friendship with Bobby going?"

"It's okay," I said, answering carefully. "We've both been really busy, so we haven't seen each other much. And he's away at football camp now."

"And your friend Carole?"

"She's fine. She's away in Paris."

"Paris?"

"Yeah, that's pretty cool, isn't it? She went with her father who was posted there this summer. And she sounds like she's having a great time."

"So how do you feel with your best friends away like that all over the world?" Mr. Aniso was trying to sound casual, but I could tell he was serious underneath.

"I'm okay," I said, trying to sound casual too. "I do get a little lonely sometimes. But I'm busy, too, helping out at the gas station. And there's my friend Tim. We set up and fix people's computers." I didn't tell him the rest of the story, how Tim was really intense at times and could get on my nerves and all that. I had a lot more important things on my mind.

We were both silent for a minute, starting to eat our pizzas. But I could tell Mr. Aniso was thinking about something.

He looked up at me. "Was there anything in particular you wanted to talk to me about, RV?"

I shrugged, not sure how to begin. "I don't know. I've just been feeling kind of out of it."

"Out of it?"

"Yeah, with everyone away, I'm feeling...I don't know...like summer's not what I was hoping it would be."

Mr. Aniso was silent again, concentrating on his slice. I felt foolish. I had texted him so we'd get together to talk, but I wasn't making much sense.

"I guess I'm upset at myself too," I blurted out.

"Upset at yourself. How?"

"I've chickened out of a couple of things lately. One thing I think I should do and another thing I'm not sure about."

Mr. Aniso waited for me to continue. I told him about Ray smoking pot in the woods with his friends. And then with whatever girl he was with. "I want to do something so he doesn't get into trouble. I mean, I'm the older brother, so I guess I feel like I should protect him, but I don't know how." Then I thought about Bobby calling me innocent. "In a lot of ways I feel like my brother is way ahead of me," I added, "so anything I say he'll laugh at."

He was nodding. "Yes, that's a serious issue." We both agreed I might have to talk to my parents about Ray's behavior, even if I didn't want to. It was for Ray's sake, and his future. But Mr. Aniso also said I should try to find a good moment maybe to talk to Ray himself. Kind of give him a heads-up.

"You just have to be prepared he might rebuff you," Mr. Aniso said. "That's one of those things in life. Sometimes we have to make ourselves vulnerable in order to achieve anything. Maybe Ray will understand in the future, even if he gets upset now."

I nodded. The future. What a loaded word. How about my future? What does it have in store for me?

Thinking about Bobby again made me blush. My face got hot. And Mr. Aniso was studying me intently. I looked down, focusing on my slice, not wanting to face him.

Mr. Aniso was silent, too, concentrating on his pizza. I couldn't stand it any longer and blurted out everything that had happened with Bobby. How he was so frustrated with the pressure from his father, how he called me innocent because I wouldn't jerk off with him. And I even blurted out that he'd told me he had gay feelings too. I knew I'd feel bad about it later, but at the moment I didn't care. I just had to let everything out.

"I still feel bad about chickening out with Bobby," I repeated. "I don't think he was happy about it."

I finally glanced up, and Mr. Aniso was looking at me intently. "I don't think you chickened out," he said in a quiet voice. "Not at all. You told him you weren't ready, and that's how you felt, right?"

I nodded.

"There's nothing wrong with not feeling ready for anything sexual," Mr. Aniso added. "Sex involves deep, complicated feelings, and doing it when you're not sure or confused can create a lot of problems."

"But is the Big M—I mean masturbation—sex?" There I was, blushing again. But I've never talked about that with anyone except Bobby. "Is it sex?" I repeated.

"RV," Mr. Aniso said, giving me a let's-be-adults look I hadn't seen before. "RV. Don't rush things. Before you think about sex, think about your feelings."

"My feelings?"

"Yes, feelings come before sex. Feelings are at the bottom of sex. You might even say feelings create sex."

I tried to understand what he was saying, but I was more concerned about Bobby at the moment. "But, but I don't want to lose Bobby," I added, barely whispering. "I don't want him to be upset with me."

"You really think you might lose him?"

"I don't know."

"Maybe Bobby is confused or unsure, too, just like you. He just called you innocent to cover up his own confusion. Have you tried talking to him?"

I laughed, though I don't know where that came from since I was feeling so miserable. "You want me to talk to everybody, Mr. Aniso. That sounds so adult. I don't feel like an adult."

Mr. Aniso smiled and shook his head. "I don't think too many people feel like adults when it comes to relationships. No matter how old they are." He paused for a second, frowning a bit. "Look, I don't want to talk you off romance and sex in the future or focus on negative things. Sex can be wonderful when the time is right. When you trust someone. And, most important, when you feel ready for it yourself."

"How do you know you're ready for it?"

Mr. Aniso smiled and shook his head again. "Ahh, yes. It's a tricky one. It takes time and some—no, a lot—of self-reflection."

"Self-reflection?"

Mr. Aniso looked at me. "Tell me, RV. What do you think about when you think about sex?"

I hesitated, staring down at my pizza slice, not sure how to answer. Blushing like crazy, too, I'm sure, with the images of the guys on the ball field and other places whizzing around in my head.

"Well?" Mr. Aniso wasn't letting go of the question.

I thought about all the other questions I had about sex. What Mom and Dad might say, sermons from the priests, stories about diseases like HIV, and my crazy dreams.

I finally looked up, facing Mr. Aniso. "I'm scared," I said, so quietly I could barely hear myself.

"Scared?"

"Yeah."

"Tell me why you're scared, RV," Mr. Aniso said almost as quietly.

I told him about all those thoughts I had. And the questions that wouldn't stop. And not wanting to lose Bobby.

After I finished I realized I was looking down at my pizza again. Mr. Aniso was silent too. But I heard him say quietly, "RV, it's okay to be scared."

I looked up at him. "It is?"

"Yes. It can be scary. Like I said, because it involves a lot of deep feelings. That's why I don't want to you to rush into anything before you're ready."

"Mr. Aniso," I asked, "do you—do you think I'm innocent?"

"I do," he said, nodding. "In a good way. No. A great way. Not in the way you suppose Bobby meant it."

I must have looked puzzled because Mr. Aniso reached over, like he did that time in the hospital, and gripped my shoulder tightly.

"Remember what I told you before, RV," he said. "You're a good guy. No, a great guy. Never, ever feel bad about yourself. And don't feel bad about everything going on in your head. By asking all these questions and talking to me, you're already leaving innocence far behind. That's how it works. It's a place to start. A place a lot of people take a long time to get to. A very long time."

He stopped, removed his hand from my shoulder, and looked away. I was wondering what he was thinking about, but I was afraid to ask.

Finally, he turned back to me. "So keep asking your questions, RV. Text me anytime. And don't be afraid to talk to Bobby just like you're talking to me. Don't be afraid to tell him how you feel. Bobby sounds like a great guy, and if you tell him you're not comfortable with something, I think he'll understand." He smiled again. "And remember, sex is not just about jerking off or being gay or straight. It's about feelings, as I said before. Your deepest feelings. I know it can take a while to figure out what they are, but keep trying."

We sat at Joe's for a while longer, talking. I tried to understand everything Mr. Aniso was telling me, though I knew I'd be puzzling over some of it for a while. But it didn't matter. Even if I didn't understand it all, it was just good to be there with Mr. Aniso, talking about these things. He always makes me feel better. And maybe that is more important than anything else.

Chapter Eight

Violence Can Do Damage

Now I'm feeling bad. It was good to have the talk with Mr. Aniso, but all I can think about is that I told him about Bobby thinking he might be gay. I don't think Mr. Aniso would tell anyone, but you never know. And I had this crazy dream last night. Some hoods who were friends of Duffy and Doyle captured Mr. Aniso and forced him to tell them everything he knew about me and Bobby. And then the hoods got ready to come after us.

Like I said, crazy. My nervous side that worries about everything has completely taken over. I tried to calm down by telling myself I'm being totally irrational. Good word, irrational. Refers to your emotions, not your intelligent thinking part. Ha! My thinking part is hiding, letting my nerves take over most of the time.

Deep down what I really feel bad about is that I betrayed Bobby's confidence. I swore to him I wouldn't say anything to anybody about him and me. Bobby's even more paranoid than I am, and I sometimes think he worries too much about being gay and all that. But who am I to judge? If I were in his position maybe I'd be that paranoid too. I guess in some ways jocks do have it tougher than us run-of-the-mill nerds. Poor jocks. Ha ha.

Why am I laughing? The main thing is I betrayed my friend and broke my promise to him. Friends don't do that. I'll feel really bad when I see Bobby next. There will be this secret between us. So what am I going to do? Confess? Or keep it to myself? I don't want to think about either option. Is there a third choice?

I guess these thoughts were swirling around in my brain when I went into work at the gas station today because Ed asked me if there was anything the matter.

"No," I said, shaking my head. "Why?"

"Because you look so glum," Ed said.

Even Melissa got in on the act. "Hey, what's the matter?" she said. "I'm not that bad a boss." She even gave me a poke in the ribs to make me laugh.

Wow, I thought. When Mean Melissa tries to make you laugh, you know you're in bad shape. I better shake off these thoughts somehow and concentrate on my work. It's easy enough for me to screw something up even when I am paying attention. But when I'm like this, I better be careful. Or Melissa will turn into her mean self pretty quickly.

But I soon learned if the worst thing that happens at the gas station is having Melissa yell at me, that's nothing,

I was sweeping the floor, Ed went out back to do something, and Melissa was at the cash register. We heard the screeching of tires as a car stopped short outside. The next thing we knew a bunch of guys came in. They started taking candy and other stuff off the shelves and putting it in their pockets. I couldn't be sure but it looked like the same bunch of guys who had come in before and drove off with stuff before we could do anything. They had a few other friends with them. And they were loud, too, laughing and carrying on, and they were talking in that same foreign language, though I still wasn't sure what it was.

"Hey! Hey! What are you punks doing?" Melissa yelled.

The guys ignored her, and kept taking things and laughing.

Melissa stepped out from behind the cash register and approached one short guy who was grabbing a bag of chips. She slapped his hand so that he dropped the bag.

"Are you going to pay for that?" she demanded. All the guys stopped what they were doing and stared at her.

One of the guys came up to her. He looked like the leader of the group. He was tall and wore a leather vest that showed off his muscular, tattooed arms. "Are you threatening my little brother?" he said to Melissa. His English was perfect, without any accent.

Good ol' Melissa is not afraid of anything. She edged closer to him so that they were standing practically nose to nose. "No. I'm not threatening anybody," she said. "I'm just telling you to put it all back or pay. That's how it works."

He stared back at her without saying anything.

"Put it all back or pay!" Melissa repeated.

He suddenly found his voice. "You want me to put it all back or pay, Big Lady?" he said, mimicking her in a baby voice. "You want me to put it all back or pay?"

"Now!" Melissa said.

"I'll show you where I'll put it," he said and grabbed Melissa by the crotch.

She was about to slap his hand away, but he blocked it and took out a knife. He held the knife up to her cheek.

"Oh, don't threaten violence, Big Lady," he said, rubbing the knife against her cheek slowly. "Violence isn't good. Violence can do damage."

"Get the hell out of here!" It was Ed, who appeared at the back door. He started walking toward the guy. "Put down the knife."

The guy didn't move.

"I said, put the knife down!"

Ed came up to the guy. He turned away from Melissa and was facing Ed, holding the knife up to Ed's face.

Ed didn't move. "For the last time, I said put the knife down."

The guy didn't move either. "Or else what, Fat Man?" he sneered.

The next thing I knew, Ed had taken out a gun from somewhere and was pointing it against the guy's chest. "Or else there will be violence," he said. "And we don't want violence, do we? Because violence can do damage," he added, repeating the guy's words back to him.

Still the guy didn't move. No one moved. I could hardly breathe.

Finally, slowly, the guy lowered the knife. "Okay, you win, Fat Man. But you're a bad man, Fat Man. That's not good. We know about violence and damage too."

"Get out! Get out of here and stay away!" Ed said, moving back a few steps and waving the gun at everybody.

"Come on, let's go," the guy said, turning to his buddies. "We don't want to mess with the bad Fat Man. Not tonight."

The guys turned around and started filing out of the door. But on their way, some of them, including the guy with the knife, grabbed some other things before running to their car.

I thought Ed or even Melissa would chase after the guys. But they stayed where they were, staring after them.

We heard the car speed off. "Are you all right?" Ed asked, coming up to Melissa.

She swore. "I'm fine," she said. "Those assholes. If I see them again around here…"

"You don't have to worry while I'm around," Ed said, showing off the gun. "This will handle those spics."

Remembering how Ed had jumped down my throat the first time when I said they weren't Spanish, I kept quiet.

But it was if Ed was reading my mind. "So you're still telling me they're not spics," he said, turning to me angrily.

"I—I don't think so," I stammered.

"Then what were they?"

"I—I don't know," I said, shaking my head. I wanted to tell Ed not to be angry at me, but I didn't dare.

"Wherever they're from, I want them to stay the hell out of here! They're not messing with my livelihood!" Ed was shouting. Even Melissa looked too scared to say anything. "Next time, I just might use the gun on them," he continued. "And no one's going to stop me!"

I didn't know if that last sentence was directed toward me or Melissa, or if Ed was trying to convince himself, but I wasn't in any kind of mood to find out.

Chapter Nine

The Best-Laid Plans

I didn't sleep well last night. Kept thinking about what happened at the gas station. And had more dreams, crazy dreams. The guy with the knife hurting Melissa, Ed shooting his gun and killing the guy, another one of the gang coming after me.

I was glad to wake up and realize I was safe in my own bed. But then I couldn't stop thinking about the gas station again. What if the guys came back? Were we safe? What if the guys had guns too? What if Ed used his gun first? Would he go to jail? Could Melissa take over for him? Would the gas station close? And should I tell Mom and Dad what happened? They might yank me out of there if they knew what was going on. Is that what I want?

At first, the thought of the gas station closing made me feel good. Yay! No more work for me! More free time to enjoy summer. More time to do what I wanted to do.

But the more I thought about it the more I realized that wasn't so great. No more work meant no more money from Ed, which nicely supplements my allowance. And despite my complaining, I was starting to enjoy it, at least some of the time. Ed was funny with most of his customers and cracked good jokes. Even Mean Melissa occasionally dropped that stern face now she was getting to know me. And maybe most important, with Carole away in Paris, and Bobby away at football camp, I didn't have anyone to hang around with. Of course there's Tim and the computer business. But I'm not sure I want to deal with his bossiness.

I can't believe it. The middle of summer, beautiful sunny weather, but I'm a little bored. That's crazy. But there it is.

So I decided not to say anything to Mom and Dad. At least not for the moment. I'm a little surprised at myself, but I guess I want to continue working at Ed's, for a little while longer. Funny. It kind of makes me feel like an adult. Here I thought I was missing the good old days of summer when it was all about having fun and enjoying myself. And I guess I still do miss that a lot of the time. But feeling like an adult is good too.

Mr. Aniso told me not to rush things. I don't think I am, am I? I'm just saying feeling like an adult is good. A little intimidating maybe, but good. (Intimidating, one of my favorite words. Means something scares you. If you let them. Is that how I really feel about life? Watch that, RV. Maybe you better start using another word that's the opposite of intimidating. What would that be?)

*

Funny, from time to time the Big Guy upstairs likes to remind me He's still around and in charge. The minute I thought I was bored, He made sure to throw more things at me to keep me from getting too comfortable.

We went to Silver Beach on Cape Cod yesterday. One of our family summer Sunday outings. We've been doing it for years. We convinced Mom that on those weekends when we go to the beach, we can go to mass in our neighborhood on Saturday—get it over with, as Ray says.

Mass is not in the Mother Tongue. But then God has a lot of Mother Tongues, as Ray reminds us. God needs practice with English too. Mom shoots Ray a dirty look when he says things like that, but she gives in. She likes the beach in summer too.

So we spend all day Sunday on Silver Beach. The Cape is over an hour's drive from Boston, but worth it. I love the beach. The soft sand, the cloudless blue sky, and the sun shimmering on the water. What could be better? Oh, oh. I'm getting poetic again. But that's okay, isn't it? If you can't get poetic about one of your favorite things in life, what can you get poetic about?

I'm a pretty good swimmer too. Better than Ray, actually, who's so skinny he gets cold in the water very quickly. But to me the water at Silver Beach seems just right. Not too cold, not too warm. And when the tide is coming in the waves are great. Not huge, but enough to do a little body surfing or just floating and being rocked like a baby.

I can stay in the water for hours, dunking and diving, surfing those waves, and doing my laps. Maybe someday I can go to the beach with Bobby and see how well he swims. Wouldn't that be great if I'm as good or even a better swimmer than he is? Wow, me better at some sport than jock Bobby! It would be the opposite of intimidating; boost my confidence for sure.

Anyway, we found our spot on the beach yesterday, ready for another Sunday of fun in the sun. After a while, a bunch of guys and their girlfriends came and set up their stuff not far away from us. They were having a great time, eating, playing music, throwing a Frisbee around and going into the water together.

I couldn't take my eyes off them. The guys anyway. A few of them looked like jocks, with defined muscles and confident, easy moves. I'm not that skinny compared to Ray, but compared to those guys, I'm puny. I tried not to stare at them too often, but the more I tried to look away the more I was drawn to them. They reminded me of the jocks on the ball field, practicing, horsing around, and goofing on each other.

Why am I so mesmerized by them? Yeah, that's the word again, mesmerized. It's like these guys are a magnet, and my eyes can't resist being drawn to them. Why do I like to look at them so much? It's one of those signs of being gay, isn't it?

But here's the scary thing. One of the guys caught me gazing at him. I looked away as quickly as I could, but when I glanced back later I saw him still staring at us. And there was nothing friendly about it, either. It was an angry glare. I got scared, afraid he'd come up to us or say something to his friends.

Luckily, none of that happened, but it spoiled the rest of my day. I couldn't relax and I didn't want to take one of my walks along the water. I told myself I was being paranoid, but I couldn't help it. Images of Duffy and Doyle, the thugs from school, kept popping up in my head. I couldn't forget how they picked up that guy McGrath and threw him against the lockers for something they thought he did.

Who knew if these guys were thugs. But why take chances? Intimidated. Intimidated. That word keeps coming back to me, as if laughing at me. I've really got to find a word that means the opposite and start repeating it to myself. I just wish I could find the right word.

*

I still feel bad about what happened at Silver Beach today. I mean, I can't help staring at good-looking guys. But am I going to get in trouble for it someday? I don't want that. And why should I? There's nothing wrong with admiring someone, is there? I guess I can practice staring at girls too. Some of them are very pretty. Even Carole. She's not gorgeous or anything, with her flaming-red hair and that ski slope nose. But she's nice and fun. And I like to be with her. Maybe I can just make more of an effort to look at her. Stare at her the way I stare at those guys. And who knows? When she comes back from Paris, she'll probably have that French thing going on. Wearing European clothes and fancy perfume, and her hair done in some new way. Doesn't that make guys go wild? Maybe it will do the same thing to me.

Oh, man. I've got to stop thinking of Carole or those guys on the beach, and get with it. I've been ignoring my summer reading list for school.

Those of us who are going to be in Class III got our own reading list for the summer. Class III is sophomores in normal high school. Of course, Latin thinks of itself as special. Where they got this Class business, I don't know. But freshman are Class IV, sophomores Class III, and on to Classes II and I for juniors and seniors. Class III's summer homework is a list of three books we have to read. And then we have to choose two more books from a long list of a hundred. Then we'll have to write an essay in English class about what we read.

I don't like being told what to read. I've been reading stuff I want to read, books I've discovered, even if some people might think they're a little crazy. But this summer

I first have to read what they tell us. That's what I get for going to a competitive high school.

They say our English course this year will be about the American Dream and what it means. Good question. Are Mom and Dad living the American Dream? Am I?

I've started looking at the list of books. The first book sounds good: *The Prince of Los Cocuyos* by a guy who was a child of Cuban immigrants. He's trying to figure out his Cuban life and his American life. Good to know there are more people like me trying to figure out their old life and their new life. I'll get that out of the library tomorrow.

And then there's one called *Evicted* about people not being able to pay their rent. Scary. Glad we don't have that problem, since we own our little house. But Dad and Mom do worry about money a lot, especially Dad. I guess worrying about money is part of the American Dream too.

And then there's a play called *Ma Rainey's Black Bottom*. I've heard of August Wilson. He writes about Black people and their struggles. This one's about a Black band trying to record a new album of a singer named Ma Rainey in Chicago in the 1920s. The play is about all the troubles they have. Some of Wilson's plays have come to Boston, and I want to see the next one. Hey, maybe I can take Bobby. He can tell me what he thinks of the play and how things have changed since the 1920s. Why not? Bobby will take me to a Patriots game, and I'll take him to a play. I can tell him what I think about football, once Bobby explains the rules, ha ha.

Come on, RV. Stop fantasizing and decide on the rest of the books you're going to read. Gone are the days of *Crime and Punishment* or *The Agony and the Ecstasy*. You have to pick from the list they gave you. Some of those books don't sound bad. Like the one called *Snow in*

August. It's about an eleven-year-old Catholic who becomes friends with an older Jewish rabbi. Wow. Sounds a little like me and Mr. Aniso.

That's what's good about books. They make you feel less alone. The more I look at the list, the more I see there are other people like me in this world. Well, maybe not exactly like me, but in similar situations and with the same questions. Makes me realize maybe I'm not as totally out of it as I think I am sometimes.

*

LOL. Just when I think I'm doing okay, I get a curve ball.

Tim and I had our first computer lesson with Mrs. Winslow today. Just as I predicted, she asked a lot of beginner questions. And Tim had a hard time dealing with it.

"Why does the computer go dark like that?"

"It's on sleep mode."

"Sleep mode?"

"Yes."

"My, my. So now computers need sleep, like people."

"Look, Mrs. Winslow, if you don't like it going dark so often, we can do something about it."

Tim made a few quick clicks while I looked on.

"Here," he said, trying to get Mrs. Winslow to focus on the place he was pointing to on the screen. "See these settings? If you don't like the screen going dark so often, we can change this setting. Right now it's on one minute. Do you want to change it to two minutes? Or five minutes?"

"You mean for it to stay dark that long?"

"No, no. It's how long it stays light and *then* goes dark if you don't touch it."

"Well, I don't know." Mrs. Winslow looked puzzled. "What about at night? I don't want it to be light at night. I want to make sure it stays dark."

"Well then, we turn it off for the night. Like this."

Tim turned the computer off, waited for a short while, and then turned it back on.

"In the morning you turn it back on," he continued. "Just like I did now."

Mrs. Winslow shook her head. "I tried that, but it doesn't always work. Last night the computer turned on by itself. It got me so scared."

"The computer doesn't just turn on and off by itself."

"I tell you it did. I thought there was an intruder in the house. I was terrified."

I could see Tim getting more and more exasperated. "Look," he finally said, glancing at his watch. "I just remembered I have to do an errand for my mother. So I have to go. But RV will stay here and answer all your questions."

Oh really?

Before I or Mrs. Winslow could say anything else, he left.

I did stay, and I tried to answer Mrs. Winslow's questions as best I could. She complained about not liking the mouse because of her arthritis, so I showed her how to use the track pad. And when she complained she had a hard time reading the screen, I adjusted the font size and the brightness.

Then she said she wanted to go on Amazon to do some shopping. I shook my head. I realized I'd already been there over an hour. I was starting to lose patience, too, and was still annoyed at Tim for leaving me alone with her. So I told her as nicely as I could that Amazon would have to wait for our next lesson.

I texted Tim as soon as I left Mrs. Winslow's house.
Why did you leave me alone with her?
Sorry, was busy.

I was about to tell him that wasn't true when another thought struck me. I told him since I was there for most of the hour with her, I should get all of the money for today's lesson. What did Carole say when we started the business? That a good businessman needs to negotiate. Well, I was negotiating. For myself. So I texted Tim about that too.

I didn't hear back from him.

Some business we're running. I thought about texting Carole again and telling her about what had happened. But again I stopped myself. Let her enjoy those croissants and those French guys.

But I promised myself to bring it up with Tim at Mrs. Winslow's next lesson. What did Mr. Aniso say? Don't be afraid of my feelings? And my feelings tell me I was gypped. And that Tim is acting too bossy.

LOL. I guess Mr. Aniso is right. Feelings are at the bottom of a lot of things. Not just sex. And I have to learn to listen to them.

*

What do they say about best-laid plans? I talked to Ray after dinner. Well, at least I tried. I don't know what made me do it. Maybe it was my feeling a little bit like an adult these days. Or maybe I really am tired of that word—intimidated.

Ray can certainly make you feel that way. When he gets angry, he's scary, almost as scary as Dad. I hate it when the two of them fight, and just want to leave the room. And I know Ray doesn't think much of me. He hangs around with the cool kids. And he thinks of himself as cool. And me? As far as he's concerned, I'm a hopeless dweeb. I know that. I think of myself as a dweeb, too, but maybe not always. Not hopeless. That's what Mr. Aniso has been trying to teach me. Maybe it's working a little bit.

The door to Ray's room was partially open, and I saw him doing his thing, lying on his bed with his headphones on, listening to music. At least he didn't steal these headphones, not like the ones we suspect he took last year at school. These aren't as good, but he bought them with his allowance money, though I think Mom helped a little bit. Hey, I don't begrudge him his headphones. If they make him happy and he bought them with his money mostly, that's fine.

I knocked but didn't wait for him to say "come in" because I figured he wouldn't hear me anyway. So I just walked in slowly and sat at the edge of his bed.

For someone his age Ray is pretty tall. And even though he's skinny he's intimidating. (That word again!) And he's got dark hair and dark eyes, just like Dad, so when he looks at you it's not a comfortable look, let me put it that way. And that's what he was doing now. Staring at me, not taking off his headphones. But he did stop tapping his fingers to the beat of the music, which he'd been doing before.

Finally, taking his time, he did take off the headphones.

"What's up?" he said, which for him is a pleasant greeting.

"Hi, Ray," I said.

"Hi. What's up?"

"Nothing's up. Just wanted to come by."

He continued looking at me, not saying anything.

"I—ah, came by to see how you're doing," I stammered, not sure how best to start.

"I'm doing fine. You?"

"I'm doing okay."

"Since Carol and Bobby aren't around, I have a little extra time, so I thought maybe we could do something together."

"Like what?"

"Oh, I don't know. See a movie or do a bike ride. Or just take a walk together. Like to the woods, and catch up. It's so nice there."

"Yeah, it is." I could see Ray thinking about something.

"There's a big rock I really like. You climb on top and you can see the countryside and hills in the distance. I love that view. It makes me feel good."

"Sounds nice."

"Do you know that rock?"

"No."

"Maybe I can show you?"

"Yeah, maybe."

This isn't going anywhere, I said to myself, as Ray kept looking at me silently. *If I'm going to say something I have to say it now.*

"Actually, maybe you do know the rock," I said, taking a deep breath. "A few days ago I was sitting on it, and I thought I heard you with some friends, so you were in the woods, too, not far away."

"Oh?"

"Yeah, I think it was last Tuesday. It sounded like you guys were laughing and having a good time. And, ah, you were smoking something too."

Ray moved up in his bed a bit, sitting up a little straighter.

"Why do you say that?"

"Because I could smell it. It smelled like pot."

"That wasn't us."

"Ray, I heard your voice. I know what your voice sounds like."

A little fear passed over Ray's eyes. "You're not going to snitch on me and tell Dad, are you?"

"No. If I was going to, I would have done that already, wouldn't I?"

The scared Ray was gone, and now the angry Ray was taking over.

"So why are you telling me now?" he wanted to know.

"Well, I'm a little worried. I don't want you to get in trouble."

"Don't worry, I won't get in trouble."

"How often do you smoke?"

"Hey, you're not my parent, so lay off me, RV."

"Ray, I'm your brother and I care about you."

"Good. Then don't bother me."

"Ray—"

"RV, have you ever tried pot?"

I didn't like feeling on the defensive. "Ray, I know some of the people you were smoking with," I said, "and they're bad news."

"Oh, so you were spying on us?"

"No I was not! I was just sitting there minding my own business, and then I heard voices."

"So you should have continued minding your own business!"

"Ray, I'm your brother and—"

"And I'm yours!" Ray said, interrupting me. "So lay off me! If anyone's going to get me into trouble, it's you!"

"No I'm not! It's the last thing I want to do!"

"So don't be an asshole and leave me alone!"

I stood up and threw up my hands. "I'm not the asshole, Ray, you are! A stupid asshole! If you don't watch it you'll end up in deep shit, and there will be hell to pay. If you want to screw up this crazy family more, go for it!"

With that I turned around and stomped out of the room.

I went to my own room, angry at myself for trying to talk to Ray. Did I make things worse? Mr. Aniso had warned me Ray might not want to listen to me, and he was right. So was I stupid for trying? When do you stop trying if there's a chance you can make things worse?

Chapter Ten

This Country Is Not for Me

Well, both Mom and Dad passed the background check and the fingerprinting part of the citizenship process. Dad complained that it felt humiliating, being fingerprinted and photographed, treated like a common criminal, with the fingerprints sent to the FBI. Mom took it differently, saying they had to do that to try to keep real criminals out of the country.

She did agree it could get really unpleasant for some people. There was a man there before them who started screaming and yelling because the FBI said there was something wrong with his fingerprints and he had to come and do everything all over again. What could be wrong with someone's fingerprints? I don't blame the guy for being upset. He had already waited for months to get his results and now the process would be delayed again. Mom said he was so upset he made Mom and Dad wait too.

Luckily, Mom and Dad's fingerprints were okay. They've received the letter saying they have been scheduled for the next step: the interview with the immigration officer. This will take place later in August. That's the biggie. That's where the officer interviews you, makes sure you can write and understand English, and can ask you any ten of up to a hundred questions about the US government and history.

Dad's nervous about this part. His English isn't great, and Mom and I are always helping him with his spelling on any forms he has to fill out. And the test depends on the interviewer. Dad showed me the test-prep booklet. Some of the questions are pretty easy, like "What's the capital of the United States?" and "How many senators are there?" But some of those questions on the test are much harder, questions I would probably get wrong. Like "How many amendments are there to the US Constitution?" and "Name one of the writers of the Federalist Papers?" Huh?

Dad claims the test is rigged. I'm not sure about that. But I guess it depends on how hard the examiner wants to make it. And with Dad's charming personality, I can see an examiner making it very hard. Dad better be on his best behavior or else.

After dinner tonight Dad asked me to help him prepare for the test. Yay! He's finally stopped procrastinating. When I walked into his little study he was flipping through the test-prep booklet. But he didn't look like he was studying. Instead he was turning the pages haphazardly and frowning. No, scowling is more like it. That's more powerful than frowning, right? Kind of like frowning to the umpteenth power.

When he saw me he put the book down and started complaining again. About a lot of things. He told me that the immigration process was all a money-making racket. That it showed the country didn't really want immigrants. That trying to become a citizen the honest way was foolish because there were easier, dishonest ways to do it. That he'd never learn all the questions no matter how hard he tried.

I just stood there not knowing what to say. Dad just can't help himself, can he? Why does he get into his complaining mode so easily? We get so sick of it. And I knew what he'd say next—that he might just pack his bags and go back to the Old Country.

"Good. Then go!" Mom says when she gets exasperated with him at times like this. Ray and I aren't brave enough to say anything. Correction. I'm not brave enough to say anything. Ray isn't afraid. Of course he often gets a good wallop for talking back to Dad, but maybe the pleasure of talking back outweighs any physical pain he feels on his ass.

Dad suddenly stopped talking as if he noticed me for the first time. He took a deep breath, asked me to sit down, and handed me the prep booklet. *Good, at least he's going to try,* I said to myself.

He told me to ask him some questions. I found the pages with test questions and we started. I tried to ask Dad easy questions first, to give him a boost. Questions like "Who's the current President?" and "What's the ocean on the western side of the United States?"

Dad got those questions right. Progress! But he's got a long way to go because when we got to the harder questions, he either shook his head or gave the wrong answer. I can see I'll have my work cut out for me for the rest of the summer. Another little chunk of summer gone. It feels weird, like I'm the parent and Dad is the child. But I do want both Mom and Dad to become citizens, so Dad will stop talking about going back to the Old Country.

Dad was quiet again after he couldn't answer the harder questions. He was staring off into space, not looking angry anymore. Instead he looked lost. I didn't know what to do. I wanted to leave and I didn't. Here was this big guy I'm usually so afraid of looking like a little kid. A lost little kid.

"*Ar nori sustoti?*" I asked. "Do you want to stop?" I told him we could continue another time.

He looked at me. "*Nežinau.*" "I don't know." He kept staring at me, but he wasn't really focusing on me. It was as if he was looking through me, focusing on something far away. I asked him again if he wanted to stop.

He ignored my question and shrugged. "*Gal šitas kraštas ne man.*" "Maybe this country is not for me." He kept repeating it. "*Gal šitas kraštas ne man.*"

He stopped and asked me what I had just said. I told him I didn't say anything. I was just waiting for him to continue. He nodded and told me to ask him some more questions. But I could tell he wasn't into it, and he kept getting most of the answers wrong.

I don't know how long we both stayed there going over that dumb booklet. Dad's thoughts were somewhere far away and we didn't make much progress.

I finally mumbled something like, "Okay, I've got to do things for Mom. We can continue this another time."

He nodded, still staring out into space. I slunk out of room, glad to leave.

But I was still thinking about Dad. Seeing him so sad got me really upset. I had never seen him like that. I felt bad for him. And for me too. Dad and I would have to work extra hard to pass that test. I'm determined to work as hard as we need to. There is no way I'm going let him take us back to the Old Country. I'm still struggling to fit in here in my own country, which is hard enough.

*

I went into the kitchen to get something sweet to help me get over the dark thoughts about Dad. Mom was on the phone with her friend from work again. They were talking about the jewelry business they were going to open. But Mom didn't look happy. Instead she seemed very upset.

From what I could tell, her friend was backing out of the deal. Mom kept asking her to reconsider, kept redoing the figures on that pad she had with her, but it didn't sound like she could convince her friend to change her mind.

She finally hung up the phone. I asked her what happened. She told me her friend had become scared about taking her savings out of the bank and investing them in the store. It turned out she had a little less money than she thought she had, and she didn't want to totally deplete her savings.

I was trying to think of something to positive to say to Mom to make her feel better, but I couldn't think of anything.

"*Kodėl toks nuliūdes?* Why are you so sad?"

But that wasn't me asking Mom. That was Mom asking me.

I told her I was sad for her. She shook her head, telling me not to let her troubles get me down. She smiled, even though her sadness hadn't gone away. She said this was a temporary setback, and she would look for other ways to get her jewelry business going again. I asked her how her online business was going, and she shook her head, meaning it wasn't. I told her Tim and I could help her with that, but she said she wanted a "real" store, and that she'd just keep trying until things worked out.

I asked her what kept her being so positive.

She shrugged and said she had seen people suffer many worse things in life, so this was nothing. She assured me she'd find another way to sell her jewelry. She wasn't going to dwell on this little setback.

She was staring at me hard while she said this, as if she was daring me to contradict her. Who am I to contradict her, even if I have my doubts? I should be happy Mom's so positive. Makes me feel better about the future. I'm just amazed she is, especially when I compare her to Dad. Does she just have different genes from Dad? Or is it something else in her personality or her previous life in the Old Country?

Mom asked me again why I looked so sad.

I admitted I had dark thoughts of my own. I told her about being with Dad and how I could see passing the citizenship test wouldn't be so easy for him. Then I asked her if there was a chance he'd go back to Europe and would try to take the rest of us with him.

Mom assured me it wouldn't happen. She told me, yes, he complains a lot, but deep down he wants to stay in this country. That he knows the code, even if he struggles with it sometimes.

The code? She repeated it for me. *"Nulenk galva, dirbk sunkiau negu visi kiti, ir daug nekalbėk. Taip gali gyventi."* "Keep your head down, work harder than anybody, and don't say much. That's how you get by."

I told her I wasn't so sure Dad really felt that way. When he looked so despondent and kept repeating that this country was not for him, he looked beat up, like he'd given up on life.

Mom shook head. *"Nesirūpink,"* she said. "Don't worry." Since I still didn't look totally convinced, she reminded me she and Dad had seen much worse things in life.

I asked her what things.

"*Blogus dalykus.* Bad things," she said. Her eyes glazed over, as if she was somewhere else. "*Mačiau blogus dalykus. Tėvas irgi.*" "I saw bad things. Dad too."

I kept quiet, wondering what these bad things were, not sure if I wanted her to continue or not.

She snapped back to the present, grabbed me by both arms, and shook me. Looking right at me, she told me a phrase she repeated when she was my age. "*Reikia būti stripriems. Reikia būti stipriems.*" "We have to stay strong. We have to stay strong." She said those words got her and her family through a lot of bad times. Sometimes she still repeats them. And she told me to repeat them too.

I did, though not with the conviction she had in her voice.

I said them a second time, trying to do better, but she had let go of me and was not paying attention. She was looking off into the distance the way Dad does.

Standing there, feeling awkward, I didn't know what to say next. But she finally turned back to me and smiled. "*Nesirūpink,*" she said again, giving me a hug. She reminded me that things are not nearly as bad now and she doesn't have to say the words nearly as often.

"*Gerai?*" "Okay?" she asked.

"Okay."

She smiled again, telling me to sound more confident. That between both of us we'd help keep Dad strong, too, and not let him take us back to the Old Country.

Chapter Eleven

Bobby's Back

Bobby's back! I'm so glad because it's been such a boring time. Ray's been his old leave-me-alone self, and Carole hasn't texted me in almost a week. That's probably because she's having such a *merveilleux* time. She keeps using that word, saying how marvelous everything is. Good for her.

Ed's Garage has been quiet too. The hoods haven't returned, which is good. But Ed and Melissa have been kind of—I don't know, different. I don't know if they're still thinking about what happened or are worried about the future. I haven't wanted to ask them.

I guess one good thing is that both Mom and Dad are in decent moods. Oh, I can tell they're thinking about the citizenship interview in August, but they're not fighting about it. Dad's starting to really study for it, which is great. He asks me to help him sometimes, but that's okay since I've had some time on my hands.

But now that Bobby's returned from football camp, Dad better give me a break. Just knowing Bobby is back makes me feel less alone, even though I have to wait two days to see him. I've invited him to my house, hoping we can sit around for a while and catch up. Then maybe we can take a walk to the woods or do a bike ride somewhere. Just being with Bobby will be nice. Like I said, just knowing he's back makes me feel less alone.

*

The two days felt like a month, but I survived. Bobby and I decided to meet in our favorite spot in the woods behind the ball field.

We climbed up onto the rock and looked out into the distance.

"So how was football camp?" I asked.

"It was good. Lots of good drills," Bobby said, nodding. "I learned some useful things and know what I have to practice." He took out some peanuts he had brought with him and shared them with me. "The rest of the summer is going to be very busy. I'll be practicing a lot." He gave me a conspiratorial look. "Tryouts for the varsity football team are in August. I'm going to go for it."

"You are? They allow sophomores on the varsity team?"

"Yeah. If they're good enough. And I plan to practice hard the rest of the summer."

I didn't know what to say, as I could see Bobby's thoughts were very much still on football camp.

"There are so many good players out there," he continued, his expression serious. "If I want to make the varsity team this coming year I really have to devote a lot of time to training."

"Are you still going to work for that accountant?" I asked.

"I had another fight with my father about that. What else is new?" He threw a peanut into the air and opened his mouth to catch it. "He still wants me to work for the guy," he continued, eating the first peanut and throwing another one into the air. "I told Dad I just don't have the time."

"Is he insisting?"

"Yeah, but I'm insisting too. So we're at a stalemate." Bobby shrugged. "We'll see who wins. How about you? Are you still helping out at Ed's Garage?"

"Yeah." I told Bobby about the incident with the guys stealing things and giving us a hard time and Ed bringing out the gun.

"Wow," Bobby said. "I've heard about those guys. They're part of two new gangs on the other side of town. You don't want to mess with them."

That made me feel great. Something else to worry about.

Bobby smiled, seeing the look on my face. "Hey, I didn't want to make you feel bad. It's okay. I'm sure Ed knows how to take care of himself. The garage will be fine." He put his arm around my shoulders and gave me a nice little squeeze. "Oh, RV. It's good to see you. I missed you."

"I missed you too," I said.

"You know, I met a lot of great guys at camp, but I thought about you a lot."

"You did?"

"Yeah, sure. Didn't you think about me?"

I nodded. If I hadn't already started blushing, I knew I was blushing now. My last conversation with Mr. Aniso and how I blurted everything out was there in my mind front and center.

"What's the matter?"

"Nothing's the matter."

"C'mon," he said, poking me in the ribs. "I know you pretty well by now. What's up?"

"What do you mean?"

"It's written all over your face." Bobby leaned in close to me. "All over your red face."

"You know I blush easily."

"Yeah, but now you're so red you're almost purple."

"No."

Bobby poked me again and tickled me. "C'mon, RV. What's up?"

"Ow!" I said, trying to get Bobby back. "That tickles."

"It's supposed to tickle," Bobby said, not letting go of me. "I'm not stopping till you talk to me."

"Okay, okay," I said. "Stop. I was just thinking about Mr. Aniso."

"What about Mr. Aniso?"

"Well, since everyone was away, you and Carole, I was feeling kind of out of it, so I invited him to Joe's Pizza."

"Really?"

"Yeah. And we had a nice conversation."

"About what?"

"Oh, just about the stuff we usually talk about, life and things. He always makes me feel better."

"That's nice."

"Yeah." I knew I had to say something. I just couldn't keep that secret. "Bobby..." I started hesitantly, looking down, afraid to meet his gaze. "Bobby, I was feeling bad that day, and I told Mr. Aniso everything about us."

"What do you mean everything?"

"Well, how I was missing you. And how we were dealing with a lot of things. And including that we might be gay."

"You told him that?" Bobby's voice was now sharp, not at all playful the way it had been just a few seconds before.

"Yeah," I mumbled. "I don't know why I said it. It just all came out."

Bobby's entire body grew stiff.

Feelings of guilt washed over me, as I remembered the details of the conversation. "I—yeah. I'm, I'm sorry I told him everything."

"You mean about the gay stuff?"

"Yeah. I was feeling so low and I needed to talk to someone and—"

I finally glanced up at Bobby but looked down quickly again because his expression was so stern.

"RV, you broke your promise."

"I know. I'm sorry. I—"

"You know what will happen if anyone on the football team finds out about us," Bobby said, not waiting for me to finish.

"Mr. Aniso wouldn't say anything."

"How can you be so sure?" Bobby frowned, and I could see he was getting upset. "Do you know how many fag jokes I heard these last couple of weeks? And I'm not talking about the players only. Some of the coaches are assholes too. Dealing with that is not fun."

"But there are gay jocks who are out these days," I said, trying to justify myself somehow. "Is it still so bad?"

"Yes, it's still bad." Bobby was staring at me. "Competition is tough. Plus I'm black. Some assholes will use any excuse." He shook his head. "Shit. Who knows if I'd still be on the team if one of the assholes found out about us."

"I'm sorry" was all I could say, growing more miserable by the moment.

"Yeah. Sorry is easy to say. But it's harder to concentrate on the football when I have to worry about fag jokes and the reaction of racist assholes. How could you do that?" He looked as miserable as I felt.

I wanted to cry.

"RV, I thought I could trust you," Bobby continued. "I guess I can't." He shook his head. "I'm sorry. I gotta go." He jumped off the rock and started to walk away.

"Bobby, I know you can trust Mr. Aniso," I said, calling out after him, trying one more time to reassure him.

"I'm glad you're so confident about it," Bobby answered, looking over his shoulder. "I wish I could be."

Then he turned back around and without saying goodbye, he disappeared from view.

I sat there motionless for a long time, stunned, ashamed, and scared. What had started out as a celebration had turned into a nightmare. I didn't want to think about anything or do anything. I just wanted to go somewhere to hide, and stay hidden forever.

*

"I tried to tell Bobby that you would never say anything, but he was still upset."

I was at Joe's Pizza with Mr. Aniso, telling him what happened with Bobby. I had contacted him again, asking if he wouldn't mind meeting me. I just had to figure out how to apologize to Bobby, and Mr. Aniso was the only person I could talk to about it.

"I feel terrible," I continued. "Bobby accused me of betraying him. I guess I did."

"Betrayed is a pretty strong word," Mr. Aniso said.

"Well, isn't it true?"

Mr. Aniso thought for a bit. "I don't think so," he finally said. "I think of betrayal as done consciously by someone, to get the person in trouble, or caught, or harmed in some way. You weren't trying to do any of those things. You were just full of feelings you had to share with someone."

I could tell he was choosing his words carefully. But if they were meant to make me feel better, he wasn't succeeding.

"You never meant to harm Bobby. Did you?" Mr. Aniso was saying.

"Of course not."

"Well, then. I wish you wouldn't think of what you did as betrayal."

"So how should I think of it? Bobby did ask me not to say anything to anybody. And I promised I wouldn't. But I did, to you. So I broke my promise to him."

"Yes. But when you texted me last week, asking that we get together, did you think, 'Oh, I want to see Mr. Aniso because I want to tell him about Bobby?' Well, did you?" he asked when I didn't reply.

I shook my head. "No."

He didn't say anything, letting me think about his reasoning.

"Okay," I said grudgingly. "So I didn't betray Bobby. But I still broke my promise to him. And he's still mad at me, so nothing has changed. Whatever we call it."

Mr, Aniso didn't say anything. He just kept looking at me, as if he expected me to continue.

"Oh, I wish I'd been able to talk to you, Mr. Aniso, while leaving Bobby out of it!" I blurted out. "I don't want to lose him as a friend. I like him a lot. And I feel so bad he's so upset."

"Can you call him?" Mr. Aniso asked.

"And say what?"

"What you just said to me."

I blushed. "I can't remember what I said."

"Try."

I fell silent. Mr. Aniso wasn't letting me get away with that one.

"Well. Okay... I told you I wish I'd been able to talk about being lonely without bringing Bobby into it."

"Which is kind of hard to do because Bobby is the main reason you were feeling lonely. Right?"

"Right," I agreed, almost in a whisper.

"And what else did you tell me?"

"That I feel so bad I've hurt Bobby. I'd like to apologize to him. Because I never meant to hurt him because I like him too much."

"And you don't want to lose him as a friend, right?"

"Of course not."

"There you go," Mr. Aniso said. "Everything we just talked about. Can't you say it to him? Or at least some of it?"

"I can try."

"Good."

"But I'm scared."

Mr. Aniso thought for a second and then asked, "Do you know who Eleanor Roosevelt was?"

"Eleanor Roosevelt? Yeah, she was a president's wife."

Mr. Aniso nodded. "Right. President Franklin Roosevelt's wife. She crusaded for the rights of disenfranchised people in the 1930s and '40s."

I nodded, too, wondering where this was going.

Mr. Aniso looked at me with that same determined expression he had when he would grab my arm hard and would tell me to believe in myself. "You know what she said?"

"What?"

"Do one thing every day that scares you."

"Easy for her to say. She was the President's wife."

Mr. Aniso didn't say anything. Just kept looking at me.

"So what if I do talk to Bobby? What if Bobby stays angry?"

"It's a chance you have to take."

"Easy for you to say."

Suddenly Mr. Aniso didn't seem so determined. He became quiet for a second and then shook his head. "You're right. I'm sorry, RV, I shouldn't have been so...so cavalier about it. It is hard. And scary. But when you care about someone, it's important not to let being scared get in the way. Because that person is too precious to lose."

Becoming quiet again, Mr. Aniso got that faraway look in his eyes. It was the same sad expression I'd seen on his face a few times when he remembered something from his past. And the same sad expression Mom and Dad had when they thought about the past.

It scared me a little, but I had to ask Mr. Aniso what was on his mind. "Are you thinking about your friend in the seminary?" I wanted to know.

He nodded. "Yes. There were things I wanted to say to him before I left. But I never did."

Mr. Aniso stared off somewhere far away, and I felt bad for him.

We both sat there quietly. I started thinking about myself in the future. Would I be sitting somewhere with that same sad faraway look, thinking about Bobby? Was regretting things in the past part of being an adult?

I didn't want to be like that. At least not yet. Not about Bobby. I couldn't let being scared make me lose someone who meant so much to me. But even as I made my decision, I grew nervous just thinking about the conversation Bobby and I would have. Why was it so hard to talk to someone when you really cared for them?

Chapter Twelve

Guns

"How many cylinders does this car have, RV?"

"Eight."

"Where are the spark plugs?"

"Here."

"And the carburetor?"

"Here."

"Very good. You're doing well, RV. Next summer I'll let you help me tune up an engine. There are some really special cars that come through here. Would you like that?"

"Sure," I lied, not wanting to displease Melissa. She has started giving me lessons about cars. Not that I asked her. Dad has been doing the same thing for years. But I just can't get into motors. Give me a book, or the chance to sit on my rock in the woods and look out at the mountains. That's what I call a good time. But motors?

Can't get away from them, though. Especially with Melissa around. She's really into them. Good for her. She'll have her own garage someday, I'm sure of it.

She started to tell me about some fancy foreign car that was being brought in by some rich guy over the weekend. Her eyes got wide with excitement as she started describing the transmission. Listening to her is almost as bad as listening to Tim talk about hard drives and processors.

"Wow! Really? Cool!"

What else do you say to someone who's excited about a car transmission?

We heard some commotion coming from the store out front. Shouts and laughter. The voices sounded familiar. Oh, oh. I knew who they were.

The guys speaking that strange foreign language were back. They were running through the aisles grabbing bags of chips and other food while shouting things to each other and laughing.

Suddenly Ed appeared. "What the—?" he exclaimed. "Get the hell out of here!"

I recognized the guy who had pulled the knife the last time. He just laughed and continued grabbing things.

"I said get the hell out of here! And pay for what you took!" Ed shouted even more loudly.

Some of the guys stopped, not looking sure what to do. The head guy with the knife stopped, too, and turned around to face Ed.

"Oh, yeah, man?" he said with a sneer. "Maybe you should get the hell out of here." He dropped the bags he had taken and approached Ed. "I said maybe you should get the hell out of here, Fat Man," he repeated. "Or there might be damage."

Ed stared at him for a second and then started to reach into a pocket of the vest he had on.

"Hold it!" yelled the head guy, whipping out a pistol.

Ed was standing there, not moving. "So, Fat Man," the head guy said. "You were going to take out your little gun." He laughed. "Okay, take it out."

Ed didn't move.

"I said, take it out!" the guy snarled. "Slowly."

Ed slowly pulled out his gun, keeping it pointed down. There they were, standing inches away from each other, Ed's gun pointing down, the guy's gun pointing at Ed.

The guy laughed again. "So. What should we do now, Fat Man?"

No one moved.

Then Melissa walked out from behind me. "Hey guys. Cool it," she said, trying to calm things down. "Cool it. Everybody, put your guns away and you guys just get the hell out of here."

Still no one moved.

"Come on, guys," Melissa said. "Take the stuff you want, and just go."

The head guy said something to one of his friends. The next thing I knew the friend come up behind Melissa and grabbed her. He held a knife up to her cheek.

The head guy turned back to Ed. "Okay, Fat Man. Give me your gun if you don't want your pretty lady to get hurt. I said give me your gun!" he screamed when Ed didn't move.

Ed started to hand over his gun. The head guy grabbed it and turned to one of his friends to say something. But as soon as he did so Ed lunged at him and grabbed back his gun.

They wrestled with each other and then a shot rang out. Melissa screamed and crumpled to the floor. The head guy yelled at his friends. They all rushed outside, but not before the head guy hit Ed on the side of the head with his gun. Ed stumbled back and his own gun fell out of his hands and skittered across the floor.

We heard the guys jump into their car and speed off. Ed's face was bleeding, but he recovered himself and rushed over to Melissa. She was moaning quietly. He cradled her in his arms.

"RV! RV!" he yelled.

I rushed out from behind the counter and saw a red circle of blood near Melissa's stomach.

"RV! Call the police! And an ambulance!" Ed was screaming. "Use the phone by the cash register!"

I ran over and fumbled with the phone, more nervous than I've ever been. For a second I couldn't even remember the numbers 9-1-1. Luckily, there was a blue police button on the phone so I didn't have to think. I called them and gave them as much information as I could. "Are they coming? Are the cops coming?" Ed kept yelling, not able to stop himself.

After hanging up, I walked back over to Ed and Melissa. The red stain on her stomach was bigger. "Some towels! There are towels in the bathroom! Quick!" I didn't know if Ed was yelling from fear or anger or nervousness, but he couldn't seem to stop. "And water! Get some water for Melissa! Hurry! Hurry!" he was yelling.

The next hour was a blur. I tried to do everything Ed asked for, but it never seemed fast enough. Luckily, the ambulance came pretty quickly, and the police right after them. The ambulance guys took away Melissa on a stretcher. Ed was holding a towel to his face. The police asked him if he wanted to go to the hospital, too, but he said he was fine.

Then the cops questioned us. I tried to tell them everything I remembered. It took Ed a while before he could calm down enough to start talking coherently. At one point I corrected him when he told the police the guys were speaking Spanish. I reminded him I knew a little Spanish and this wasn't Spanish. I wish I had kept my mouth shut, though, because Ed gave me such a look, I don't know if I'll be able to set foot in the gas station again.

The cops questioned me some more about the language the guys spoke. Trying to help me, they mentioned some neighboring towns where various immigrant groups were known to congregate. But I couldn't tell them much. We all had heard about various immigrant gangs and had seen news reports on TV about crime, but nothing in particular stuck out. When I think about it now I'm amazed I remembered anything, given how nervous and scared I was.

I was glad when the police offered to give me a lift home because I didn't want to face Ed alone. He still seemed angry, alternately muttering curses and then stopping and looking at the towel he had used to wipe the blood from his face, before holding it back up to the side of his head. He did manage to go and retrieve his gun, telling the police it was properly registered and even showing them some paperwork.

As I left, I heard him still muttering behind me. "The bastards. This isn't the end of it. This isn't the fucking end of it!"

*

I was sitting quietly at dinner, still shaken up from what happened at Ed's Garage. One minute I wanted to blurt out everything, while the next minute I didn't want to say anything. At first Mom and Dad didn't notice. Things still seem okay between them. I'm glad. With the immigration interview only two weeks away, they're focused on that. And on Ray, who seems to be in a good mood for a change. At dinner he wasn't even looking at his cell phone, but telling them happily about what a great summer he was having.

I wonder why, I said to myself, thinking about the time I had overheard him and his friends in the woods. I wondered how often they were smoking pot, and still couldn't decide whether to try to talk to him about it again or tell Mom and Dad. But I really didn't have the energy to make any decisions about that, not at the moment.

Dad turned to me, saying he wanted to have another study session with me, promising he would do better this time. He wasn't complaining or saying anything else negative about the interview, so I guess his attitude really has changed, at least a little. Mom looked pleased.

"Sure," I answered in English, not really caring one way or the other.

"*Kas yra?*" Mom asked, turning to me.

"*Kodėl? Nieko,*" I answered. "Why? Nothing."

If anyone knows my moods it's Mom, and she told me so. She asked again why I was so glum.

I started to shake my head, but then I stopped. And it all came out. I guess I just can't keep anything in. I told them about the guys who'd been terrorizing the gas station. The guns. Melissa getting shot. Ed's reaction.

Mom reacted in horror. Dad asked how long it had been going on. Even Ray seemed interested in everything I was describing.

I answered their questions and then told them that I didn't want to go back there. That I was too scared.

It really wasn't the whole truth. It was true I was scared, and not sure those guys wouldn't come back again. But I was more scared of Ed, remembering the look he gave me when I corrected him in front of the cops, saying the guys weren't speaking Spanish. The thought of facing

Ed's angry glare again was frightening, as frightening as when Dad gets angry at us and we're waiting for him to lash out at us.

Mom and Dad supported my decision, saying that under no circumstances was I to put myself in harm's way. Ed would have to understand. Then they started talking about some of the immigrant groups who were moving into the surrounding towns and the recent headlines about new crime waves. They asked me more about the guys who terrorized Ed and if I knew the language they spoke.

I shook my head, saying no, and adding that I did know it wasn't Spanish.

Mom and Dad continued talking about the news reports of a rising crime rate in the surrounding towns and whether crime was creeping into our neighborhood. They even mentioned the possibility of moving, though they both had to acknowledge there was no money for that now. Dad got angry, saying he was frustrated to be in this position. He cursed the guys who terrorized Ed's Garage. And said something about too many immigrants coming in.

"But you guys are immigrants too," Ray pointed out in English.

"*Mes laikomės įstatymų!*" Dad answered. "We follow laws!"

"*Mes ne vandalai,*" Mom felt compelled to add. "We're not vandals."

"Not every new immigrant is a vandal." I've got to hand it to Ray. He can be a pain in the ass, but he's never afraid to talk back or bait Mom and Dad. And they were too upset about crime and the gas station to chastise him for not speaking the Mother Tongue at the dinner table.

Dad glared at Ray, but turned away, not saying anything.

Mom reminded us the citizenship interview was in two weeks. She asked Dad how his studying for the test was coming along.

Dad grumbled. Now he was back in his old bad mood I know so well. Doesn't take much. *"Čia tikra bezabrazija. Ar aš čia tikrai noriu gyventi?"* "There's chaos here. Do I really want to live here?"

Ray and I rolled our eyes. *There he goes*, I'm sure we both said to ourselves at the same time. *Bezabrazija.* Using his favorite Russian word again for chaos. And saying he doesn't want to live here.

"I'm sure there's *bezabrazija* in Russia too," Ray said, not letting up.

"Tu geriau tylėk, jeigu nenori kad aš tau duočiau bezabrazijos," Dad said, pointing to his belt and telling Ray to keep quiet.

"Nu, gerai užteks," Mom said, getting into her peacemaker role. She told Ray to keep quiet and finish his meal. She told Dad to go study some more for his citizenship interview. Dad grumbled but didn't say anything.

I left the table feeling depressed. Even though not working at Ed's Garage and getting extra hours of freedom for the remaining weeks of summer was something I was supposed to be happy about, the idea made me a little sad too. As I had already begun to realize, I was starting to like working there most of the time. Even Melissa was growing on me. Plus, getting a little money didn't hurt either.

The talk about crime and possibly moving away from here by Mom and Dad made me sad too. I don't want to move! There's Bobby. And Carole. And a lot of other good things about this neighborhood, like my special place in the woods.

I turned my anger on the gang of guys. How dare they upset my life like this!

But I found myself angry at Ed, too, for thinking he could outsmart the gang and for having a gun. What good did it do him, knocked out of his hands and sliding across the floor of the shop like that? And then there was Melissa. She was suffering most of all. What if she didn't make it? That was too terrible to think about.

I tried to relax in my room, closing the door to the world outside. But I couldn't get all those scenes out of my head. I lay on my bed and closed my eyes, trying to not think about anything. But all I could hear were Ed's words as I left the gas station.

"This isn't the end of it. This isn't the fucking end of it."

*

No sooner do you decide on something than life has other plans. How many times do I need to learn that?

I was up in my room after dinner, thinking about Bobby, trying to get the courage to give him a call. But then Ed called and asked to speak to Dad. They talked about what had happened at the gas station. Dad called me downstairs and handed me the phone. Ed told me Melissa would be okay. The bullet had not penetrated any vital organs, so even though the bleeding looked bad she would make a full recovery. Great news.

Ed asked to talk to Dad again, so I gave the phone back to him. They began talking about me. Dad said what happened was all too bad, but he and Mom couldn't let me work there anymore. Ed pleaded with him to let me come back. These weeks in the middle of summer were a busy season, he explained, and with Melissa in the hospital he really needed the help. Plus, most important, the police had promised to send a squad car over to watch the gas station and patrol the area.

After some back and forth, Dad finally said it would be okay with him only if it was okay with Mom. He gave the phone over to her. At first she said no, but Ed kept pleading. He raised other arguments, too, telling her he wouldn't be able to find a replacement as good as me on short notice. Plus he told Mom what a good worker I was and gave me a bunch of other compliments. So Mom finally said okay too—if it was okay with me.

So then the phone went back to me.

"Hi, RV. You heard what I told your Mom and Dad. I really need your help."

"Yes."

"And the police will be patrolling the area and keeping watch over the station."

"Yes."

"And I really would have a hard time finding a replacement as good as you. Not at this point in the summer."

I kept thinking of the angry look Ed had given me when we were talking to the police. He certainly didn't sound angry now, as he kept complementing me and telling me what a good worker I was. I pictured him on the phone, practically on his knees, begging me to come back.

Then came the kicker. "I'll give you a raise in your pay too," he said. "Five more dollars an hour."

Well, how could I refuse that? There went those carefree fifteen to twenty hours of freedom a week I had just gained. My summer was reverting back to its old, unsummerlike self.

"Okay," I said, a little hesitantly. "I'll do it."

"Thanks so much," Ed said, promising me everything would be okay. He told me if I ever felt uncomfortable or unsafe I wouldn't have to stay. Mom and Dad said the same thing. Then Ed asked to speak to Dad again.

I left the room while Ed and Dad were talking. I told myself I didn't really mind losing those carefree hours. I was already thinking about Bobby again. If he and I didn't patch things up, I wouldn't know what to do with all that spare time anyway. There was only so much sitting in the woods and contemplating nature one could do.

Chapter Thirteen

Something's Different

"Hi, RV. How are you doing?"

"I'm—I'm okay," I answered, stuttering. I couldn't believe it was Bobby on the other end of the phone.

"RV, I uh—wanted to apologize for some of the things I said last week. I was upset. I'm sorry."

"That's okay, Bobby. I—uh—can't blame you, I guess."

"I've been thinking about it, and I overreacted. Because, well, because I was caught off guard."

"I understand."

"Some of the guys will be okay if I'm gay, but others won't be," Bobby continued. It sounded like he needed to explain himself. "And the coach, I don't know. I just can't take that chance."

"I understand," I said again, not knowing what else to say.

"I wish I was strong enough. But I'm not. I'm just not."

I stayed silent, wishing there was something halfway intelligent I could say, but my mind was a blank. I wanted to jump up and down and yell like a fool, "Bobby is calling me! Bobby is calling me!"

Bobby was quiet too. There we were on the phone, silent, wanting to say a million things to each other, but not being able to say anything.

Finally, Bobby broke the silence. "So, do you want to get together?"

"Sure," I answered. I asked him what his schedule was.

He told me that with football practice starting, he had finally succeeded in stopping his work for the accountant he didn't like, Mr. Moocher.

"That's good," I said. "How did you get your father to agree to that?"

Bobby smiled a little. "I just kept insisting. I guess if you care enough about something, you find the energy to stand up for whatever it is you want to do."

I nodded, remembering how I had stood up to Mom and Dad about not going to summer camp. Small victories, but victories, nevertheless.

"So how are you doing?" asked Bobby. I told him about everything that had gone on at Ed's Garage.

"Wow!" he exclaimed. "Pretty intense." He paused for a minute and then asked, "How do you feel about going back to work there?"

I told him I had mixed feelings, but having the police patrolling the place made me feel better. "Besides," I added, "I don't think those guys will come back. Not after what happened."

"Yeah, I guess you're right," he agreed. Then, changing the subject, he said, "So, are you up for a slice of pizza?" He paused and then added, "My treat."

"You don't have to do that."

"It's okay. I—I want to."

"Okay, then," I answered, even though I just had lunch. But I wasn't going to tell him that.

So we agreed to meet at Joe's in a half hour.

I hung up the phone, still wanting to jump and down. So Bobby had forgiven me. And he wanted to get together. And it would be just like before. Even though the end of summer wasn't that far away, maybe the last few weeks would be the summer I always wanted. I couldn't be happier as I got out my bike and made my way to Joe's as fast as I could.

*

Except everything wasn't like before. When I walked into Joe's, Bobby was already there. He was talking to a bunch of guys sitting at a booth and sharing a pizza.

"Hi," I said, coming up to Bobby a little hesitantly.

"Hi," Bobby said. He introduced me to the guys in the booth. It turned out they were some of his football teammates who had just discovered Joe's. "I've conned RV into prepping me for my upcoming English and history classes," Bobby was telling his teammates." He chuckled. "My version of summer school. In return I will begin teaching him how to throw a good pass." He laughed again, turning to me and then turning back to his teammates. "I think I got the better end of the deal since I'm the world's worst writer and speller."

They all laughed with him. "Yeah, your Hail Marys are getting better," one of the guys teased him. "If someone actually starts catching them, I guess you can qualify as a teacher."

They all laughed again and made some more jokes. Bobby looked very comfortable with them, joking and teasing right along with them.

They invited us to join them, which was nice of them. But Bobby turned down the offer. "Nahh, thanks, guys," he said shaking his head. "We just came in to grab a quick slice. Then we have to go over a few things for school. I haven't even started on my reading list."

"Big deal. We haven't started on our reading list either," one of the guys told us.

Then another of them said, "Hey, RV. Maybe you can help me with the reading list too. My arm is better than Bobby's."

"Yeah! Great idea!" a few of the other guys chimed in.

I stood there confused, not sure if they were serious or just teasing me.

Luckily, Bobby came to my rescue. "Nope. Nope," he said to the guys. "He's *my* teacher. He's got enough work to do with me without adding you goons too. Don't want to overload the guy and give him a nervous breakdown." And he practically pushed me toward the counter to get our slices as he said goodbye to his teammates.

"Thanks," I said as we sat down with our slices.

"For what?"

"I don't know. For rescuing me from those guys."

"They're not bad guys," Bobby said. "They were just kidding around."

"I know," I said, nodding. "I just—I just don't know how to be around guys like that." The word intimidated came into my mind again. I gazed at Bobby. "You're so lucky. You're comfortable with them and with someone like me."

Bobby shrugged. "I'm just being myself."

"That's just it. You don't even have to try hard. You fit in everywhere. The whole world."

"Now wait a minute," Bobby said. "Don't make it sound so easy. I fit in some places, sure. But other places?" He gave me a hard stare. "Look at me. Look at me, RV."

I did as he asked but didn't say anything since I didn't know what he was getting at.

"RV. What do you see?"

"I—I see a guy," I stammered, still not sure what he was getting at.

"What kind of guy?"

"I don't know. A guy." I was starting to fidget, not sure where this was going.

"A black guy," Bobby said finally. "Don't you see a black guy?"

"Well, I suppose so. But I hardly notice."

"You hardly notice, but other people do. It's the first thing they see, and they already assume I'm some kind of person just because I'm black." Bobby was silent for a minute and then said, "Football camp was good. But one day I overheard two of the coaches talking. They were saying how black guys were good for this thing but not that thing. And black people were good in this situation but not that situation, so they had to be careful who they chose. As if every black person is all the same one person." He looked upset. "Call it what you want, RV— insensitivity, prejudice, stupidity. It exists. That's why I'm so paranoid. I feel if I just do one wrong thing or if one of the coaches finds out something he doesn't like about me, he'll have an excuse to kick me off the team if he wants."

"I understand," I said, trying to be sympathetic.

"No you don't," Bobby said. "You're white. You just can't understand that feeling."

I felt like I had to defend myself at least a little bit. "Yeah, I'm white. But my family has had prejudice too." I told him about my father being called names at work.

"It's different."

"Well, yeah, it's different, but it's still prejudice. Isn't it?"

"I guess so," Bobby answered. But I could tell his mind was still on football camp. Frowning, he was finishing his pizza slice absentmindedly.

I stayed silent, not knowing what to say. Here I was hoping to find Bobby in a good mood, so we could spend a nice day together. Instead he was off in his own world, and he didn't seem to care if he was with me or not.

We finished our slices, Bobby went to say bye to his teammates, who were still there, and then we left Joe's. Trying one last time to make it a nice day together, I asked Bobby if he wanted to go for a bike ride or come over to my house to hang out. But he didn't really seem into it. So we parted. Bobby said he'd call as soon as his schedule would allow, but warned me about his upcoming football practice.

"It's going to take a lot of my time," he said, "so I don't know when I'll next be able to call you."

"Sure," I said, "I understand." But here was another thing I didn't understand. Not really.

*

I'm trying not to feel too depressed. Can't help thinking about Bobby and our meeting at Joe's earlier today. He seems different since he got back from football camp. First he got angry at me and then he apologized. But when we got together his mind was still very much on football. More than being with me or having a nice day. He looked so happy and relaxed, joking with his teammates. Does he feel more comfortable with them? Maybe I'm wrong thinking he's happy and fits in with all types of people. Including me.

Or is all this my imagination? After all, we've only seen each other twice. Maybe I just caught Bobby at a bad time. Maybe I'm making everything up. Is this RV, the worrier, taking over again?

I've got to stop thinking about it or else it will drive me crazy. What are Mom's words? Gotta stay strong? This isn't like being tortured by Communists or fascists but, still, I've gotta remind myself to stay strong until I see Bobby again. I've got to find something else to do to take my mind off him until then, if that's possible.

*

Ha ha ha. If there's one person who can take my mind off Bobby, it's Tim. In a bad way.

We had to see Mrs. Winslow again for her second computer lesson. Who do I see coming up the street but Tim with a girl. She was short with tight curly hair and glasses, looking like one of those geniuses you see on cartoons or in comic books. When they came up to me Tim introduced her as Loretta.

"Hi, I said, extending my hand.

"Hello," Loretta said, grabbing my hand with a tight grip.

"Loretta's here to help us with Mrs. Winslow," Tim explained. "She's a wiz with hard drives and modems, and little old widows too." If that was supposed to be a joke, he wasn't smiling. Neither was Loretta.

"So, I understand Mrs. Winslow is a real beginner," Loretta asked, turning to me.

"Yes, she's a nice lady. But she does ask a lot of questions," I acknowledged.

"The nice ladies are the worst," Loretta said, looking more and more serious. "Well, let's go. See what we can do." And she began marching up to the front steps.

I turned to Tim with a confused look. *Does Carole know about this?* I wanted to ask.

Tim's always one step ahead of me, or thinks he is. "I met Loretta on a sci-fi forum," he said over his shoulder, as he started to follow her. "She's really cool. And smart. We're lucky to have her."

What was this? So she was now part of the team? "Did you check with Carole?" I couldn't help asking again, tagging along behind.

"Don't worry," Tim said. "It's all good." And he went up and stood beside her as she rang the bell.

Mrs. Winslow opened the door with her usual smile. She greeted everyone warmly and asked if we wanted milk and cookies.

"No, thank you," Loretta said, speaking for all of us. She asked Mrs. Winslow where the computer was, and Mrs. Winslow led her to it.

"So how are you doing with it?" asked Loretta, standing by the computer. "I understand it's a new set-up."

"Well, I'm just beginning to use it," Mrs. Winslow answered. "Trying to keep up and all that." She giggled. "You young people don't need to worry about that, do you?"

Loretta and Tim were all business, ignoring her giggling and asking her what issues she had with the computer.

"Issues? Well..." Mrs. Winslow looked lost for a second. Then she giggled again. "Issues. It sounds like we're talking about people, doesn't it? Oh, what will they think of next?" She turned to Loretta. "Do you think of the computer as a person... I'm sorry, I forget your name. Louise?"

"It's Loretta. And no, this is simply a machine, Mrs. Winslow," she answered matter-of-factly. "It has been programmed by engineers with various commands and algorithms to respond to our tapping of the keys. That is all."

"My, my," Mrs. Winslow said, though she looked more confused than ever.

Tim suddenly spoke up. "Okay, Mrs. Winslow. I have to go to another engagement. I'll leave you in the good hands of Loretta and RV." He excused himself and left before anyone could say anything.

Great, Tim doing his disappearing act again, as if he's the boss and we're the peons. I promised myself I would text Carole. I didn't care what handsome French guy she was running around with or what delicious croissants she was eating.

Loretta quickly took over the conversation, asking Mrs. Winslow what she had learned since the computer was set up.

"I know how to turn it on and off...I think," she said. Then she began telling Loretta about the computer turning itself on in the middle of the night, just as she had told us.

Loretta told her computers don't just turn themselves on and off.

"But this one does!" Mrs. Winslow insisted. She turned to me. "Do you think it's haunted?"

I shook my head. "Ah, I don't think so. Maybe it's some weird electronic thing."

Loretta told her she might be dreaming, as she went behind the desk where the computer was situated and started inspecting the wires.

Mrs. Winslow insisted she wasn't dreaming. "I know when I'm awake. And I know when I'm asleep," she said. "And I was awake. Hearing strange voices and seeing the strange light from this room. It was very frightening, I tell you."

Loretta didn't respond, and continued checking the wires. That left me to calm Mrs. Winslow down.

And that's how we spent most of the time with Mrs. Winslow. Loretta asked a few questions as she checked various things on the computer. I was left to comfort Mrs. Winslow, and to translate Loretta's questions and explain what Loretta was doing.

It was not fun, and certainly not like when I used to do the same thing with Carole.

"Confused little lady," Loretta mumbled as we left Mrs. Winslow's house. "I don't know why she got a computer in the first place. At her age."

I don't know how you got onto this team, but I will find out! I wanted to reply. But of course I didn't. I did remind myself, though, to text Carole and find out what was going on.

Chapter Fourteen

Comfort and Compromise at Joe's Pizza

"I don't know how I feel. I guess I feel okay, but then there are moments I feel—I don't know, weird. Yeah, weird."

"How weird?"

"Just weird. I can't describe it."

I was at Joe's Pizza with Mr. Aniso, trying to explain how I was feeling. I needed to talk about everything that had happened with Bobby. But I was doing more babbling than explaining. And good old Mr. Aniso was listening patiently.

"I'm sorry I'm not making sense, Mr. Aniso," I continued. "Sometimes every minute with Bobby makes perfect sense. Other times, like the other day, it's just, well, weird."

Mr. Aniso took a bite of his pizza, thought for a second, and then looked at me. "RV, What I want to find out," he said after another bite, "is what was on your mind after you saw Bobby. Were you bothered by something?"

"Well, I don't know... Bobby seems different."

"Different?"

"Uh-huh."

"How different?"

"Well, I'm not sure exactly. When he came back from football camp, I was expecting things between us to be like before. But they're not."

Mr. Aniso didn't say anything, waiting patiently for me to continue.

"I guess... Well...I was hoping we could have fun again, like go for a bike ride to Larz Anderson Park. Or just enjoy hanging out together." I took a bite of my pizza, thinking. "But—but Bobby is more serious now."

"How serious?"

"Just serious. He's got football on his mind. Totally. It's all about making the varsity team."

"Is that so bad?"

"I don't know." I took more bites of my pizza, not because I was hungry but because it gave me time to sort out my thoughts. I told Mr. Aniso the conversation Bobby had overheard in football camp between the two coaches and how it bothered him.

"Maybe Bobby has reason to be bothered by that," Mr. Aniso said. "He's dealing with a lot of things."

"Yes, but I am too," I answered.

"Fair enough," Mr. Aniso agreed.

Then I finally asked him the question that was really on my mind. "But—but does that mean he doesn't care about me as much?" I wanted to know. "I still care about him."

Mr. Aniso was shaking his head and looking at me kindly at the same time. "Ah, yes, RV. Welcome to relationships."

What was that supposed to mean?

Mr. Aniso smiled in a sad sort of way. "Relationships are complicated. Because people are complicated. You have a lot on your mind. Bobby has a lot on his mind. It doesn't mean you both have the same things in your mind at the same time, does it?"

"I guess not."

"So maybe making the football team is the most important thing for Bobby right now. With all the pressures he's dealing with, maybe he can't deal with anything else for the moment."

"For the moment?"

Mr. Aniso smiled again in that same sad way. "Yeah, that's the tricky part. Who knows how long the moment lasts. You have to decide how long you can accept that."

"And then what?"

"And then...well. Let's take one step at a time. As I've been telling you, don't rush anything. I think Bobby likes you, from everything you've told me. So maybe he just needs to work out his feelings about the football team and his dad first."

I sat there in silence, as usual trying to absorb everything Mr. Aniso was saying, but still feeling like there was so much more to understand.

"What's the matter, RV?" Mr. Ansio asked me.

I shrugged. "I guess I can see what you're saying, but...but I still have a lot of thoughts going around in my head."

"That's good," Mr. Aniso said. He reached across the table and gripped my shoulder, squeezing tightly. "Remember what I always tell you, RV. You're on your way to figuring things out. You're a great guy. And you will. I promise you that you will. It all just takes time."

Just then a bunch of guys came in. They were Bobby's teammates, the same guys who had been there the day before. Passing by, some of them looked at me as if they recognized me, but no one said anything. Mr. Aniso quickly jerked his hand away from my shoulder. I froze, embarrassed to be seen there with him.

The guys sat down at a booth not too far way. Luckily, I was not facing them or I would have been tempted to keep glancing over in their direction, to see if they were looking this way. I told Mr. Aniso who they were. And blushed as I confessed to him that I was a little uncomfortable they saw us together.

Mr. Aniso smiled, though the sad look was back in his eyes.

"It's okay, RV," he said. "Why do you think I took my hand away from your shoulder?" He shook his head. "You think I'm so confident in everything I do as a gay person or...heck, as just a person? But the world doesn't understand a lot of things, and we have to make adjustments. Even if we're not always proud of them."

Seeing the sadness in his eyes, I felt bad for him. I felt bad for me, too, wondering about Bobby's teammates and so tempted to turn around to see if they were watching us.

Anger flared up in me. Why was I worried about those guys? Why did Mr. Aniso jerk his hand away and look so sad? Why did we have to be in this position? Why was the world so fucked up?"

"Thanks for coming out to have pizza with me, Mr Aniso," I said. "I really appreciate it. I—I feel you're always there for me."

He smiled, though his sad expression was still there. "Thanks, RV. I'm glad. And I'm always there to talk to."

I didn't like seeing him so sad, and I wanted to comfort him. "You're right," I said. "I will figure things out. I guess it all just takes time."

"Yes, it takes time," he said. "Sometimes a very long time. Give Bobby a chance. Give relationships a chance. And give yourself a chance. Keep searching and asking questions. I'm so glad when I see you doing that."

I don't know what made me do it, but I reached over and put my hand on his shoulder, like he had done to me. And I squeezed, squeezed really hard, not caring who saw me or what they thought. I wanted Mr. Aniso to know that I believed what he told me. And just like he comforted me, I was now happy to comfort him.

*

"RV, you have to be careful."

"What do you mean?"

We were back on my favorite rock in the woods on one of those summer evenings when the sun is about to set and the light makes everything look so peaceful and calm. I'm not sure what I expected from Bobby exactly, but one thing I didn't expect was a lecture.

"What do you mean?"

Bobby thought for a second, looking uncomfortable. "Well, a couple of the guys from the team went to Joe's the other day and they saw you with Mr. Aniso."

"So?"

"So. It isn't exactly a secret that Mr. Aniso is gay."

"So?"

"Well, they saw you touching each other and—"

That made me mad. "We were not touching each other!" I felt I had to explain more. "It's just a thing we do. Grab our shoulders to...to show support. We hold on to the other person's shoulder, tight, real tight. Mr. Aniso started it when I visited him in the hospital."

"I'm sorry, RV. I'm sure you're right, but that's not how the guys saw it. People jump to conclusions."

"Yes, they do." I stared hard at Bobby and asked, "So what did they do? Warn you about hanging out with me?"

Bobby seemed surprised and even hurt by my reaction. The last thing I wanted to do was hurt him, so I backed down a little.

"I know being on the varsity team is important, Bobby. But you yourself said some of the guys would be okay with it."

Bobby nodded. "Yeah, some of the guys..."

"What did the guys who went to Joe's tell you exactly?"

Bobby looked more and more uncomfortable. "Just that...just that you and Mr. Aniso were there together..."

"And...?"

"And well... Oh, come on, RV. Mr. Aniso is gay, and people see you two together. And they see us together. So—"

"So they think Mr. Aniso or I are going to make you gay or something? What a laugh." I was surprised by my own reaction. The last thing I wanted was to be mad at Bobby, but I couldn't help it. I don't know if I was disappointed in his reaction or angry. Angry that he wasn't defending me and Mr. Aniso.

"Oh, come on, RV, don't look so mad," Bobby said. "I told you what life is like on the team. Some guys are okay with being gay and others aren't. They just aren't. And then there are the coaches."

I didn't say anything, but Bobby continued defending himself. "I told you. The last thing I want is dealing with fag jokes or knowing someone is talking behind my back. Or worse. A reason for the coaches to keep me off the team."

I knew he was right, but I was still angry, angry that things had to be this way.

"So are you saying we can't go to Joe's Pizza together anymore? Or you don't want to be seen with me if I'm seen with Mr. Aniso?"

It was Bobby's turn to be silent. There we were, sitting on that rock, me angry, Bobby brooding. The sun had set behind the hills and everything seemed much darker. Including our moods.

*

I guess I was still angry at dinner because both Mom and Dad asked what the matter was. I told them nothing was the matter, but they didn't buy it. Even Ray got in on the act, asking if I got rejected by a girl. Everyone started asking me about Carole. I said I hadn't heard from her in a while. They all joked that she probably met some romantic French guy and was involved with him. Then they started on their thoughts about romance, and how it doesn't last, which made me even more frustrated. I was about to burst out and say something I knew I would regret later, when luckily the talk turned to citizenship.

It was time for another lesson with Dad. He really had studied and knew most of the answers. And the happier he looked, the worse I felt. Here he was, happy to become a citizen of this country, while all I kept thinking about was how Bobby and Mr. Aniso were feeling, how they had to make compromises and keep from doing things they wanted to do. So was this country fair, at least to people like them? And me, too, since it affected me also? As much as I didn't want to admit it, the answer was no.

Chapter Fifteen

Why Did You Come Here?

Being back at Ed's Garage today started well. Ed was like his old self, smiling, talking to customers, cracking jokes. And there were just as many customers as usual. Even though the "incident," as it was called, made the news, people didn't stay away. I saw a cop car come by a few times and even stop for a while across the way. That made me feel better. Ed had been telling the truth when he said the police had agreed to put in extra time watching his garage.

Ed also showed me how to do some extra things and made jokes about my needing to earn my new raise. He also told me Melissa was doing okay, and that I could go along with him or go myself to visit her. I said, sure. After visiting Mr. Aniso in the hospital a couple of times, I feel like I know my way around hospitals now.

During the middle of my shift, when I was at the gas pumps, a car pulled up with two older guys in it. After they asked for gas they started talking to each other in a foreign language. I couldn't tell for sure, but it sounded like the same language the guys who kept bothering us spoke. These two guys looked a little like them, too, with grayish-dark hair and dark complexions. But they were much older, middle-aged, I guess, and one of them had a beard. I wondered if they were Muslim.

The guy with the beard got out of the car and went inside to the garage store. I finished pumping the gas, and the guy at the wheel paid me. Since the other guy was still in the store I asked this guy if he wanted his windshield cleaned. He said sure, so I did that. When I finished, the other guy still hadn't come out of the store. With no other customers driving up, I decided to go back inside.

I heard loud voices as soon as I opened the door. The guy with the beard was standing at the counter facing Ed, who was at the cash register. There were a few bags of food and other stuff on the counter. They were arguing.

"I gave twenty. Not ten," the guy with the beard said in a slightly accented voice.

"No. You gave me ten, and I gave you a dollar thirty, so we're done," Ed said in a determined voice. And he wasn't smiling.

"Sir, you are wrong. I gave twenty. See my wallet. No twenty," the guy said, opening his wallet and showing Ed.

"I told you we are done!" Ed said, getting red in the face. "You did not give me twenty!"

"You are cheating me!" the guy yelled.

"No! You are trying to cheat me!" Ed yelled back. "Now get the hell out of here, you—"

At that moment, his eye caught my eye, and I bet he was going to call the guy a spic. But instead he stopped himself and said, "Wherever the fuck you're from! I said get the hell out of here!"

"I live here in town! That's where I'm from!" The guy said something in a foreign language that sounded like a swear. Then he slammed his hand down on the counter, scattering some of things he had bought onto the floor.

Ed started fumbling for something underneath the counter. *Oh no!* I thought. *Here we go again.*

"If you don't leave this second I will call the police!" Ed was yelling.

"I will call the police too! You bastard!" the guy yelled back. He swatted the rest of the things on the counter onto the floor, turned around, and strode toward the door.

Then he turned around again. Pointing a finger at Ed, he yelled, "And I will make sure everyone know this is cheating place! You will lose business! Much business!"

He turned around again and hurried out of the door, without taking any of the things he had bought.

Ed was standing still behind the counter, turning more and more red-faced. I slowly started picking the things up off the floor.

We heard the car doors slam shut and the car speed off.

"They're gone," I said quietly, putting some of the bags on the counter. Ed was staring straight ahead, not moving, not saying anything. He was still very red-faced, and his lips were trembling.

I then made myself busy by putting the things back where they belonged. Ed started to mumble. "I can't take this. I can't take this anymore!" he was saying.

"Was he trying to cheat you?" I asked, to make conversation.

"C'mere! Look!" Ed said. He motioned me to the cash register and opened it.

"Do you see a twenty-dollar bill here?"

"No," I answered.

"And don't tell me he might have made a mistake or gave me two tens!" Ed said. I'm glad I didn't say anything, though the thought crossed my mind.

Ed couldn't let it go. "I can see you want to defend him. It's written all over your face!" he said accusingly.

I had to answer back. "I'm not defending him," I said. "I just don't know if he did try to cheat you or not."

Ed didn't like that answer. "What is it with you kids?" he continued. "You want to be so open and understanding. You see what that gets you. I don't care if they're spics or Muslims or Eskimos from some other Godforsaken place. I don't want people like that here. I don't want to be cheated!"

I tried not to say anything as I finished putting all the scattered stuff back where it belonged. But I must have shaken my head without even realizing it because Ed called me on it.

"Why are shaking your head, RV? What I said is so bad?"

He wasn't yelling any longer, so I felt compelled to answer. "I don't think every person who comes here from another country is like those young guys."

"But some of them are, aren't they?" Ed shot back.

"Yeah, but some of us Americans are criminals too," I answered. "Doesn't mean all of them are."

"Why are you giving me that PC stuff?" Ed said. He was still upset, but he sounded a little less angry.

I guess that made me feel bolder, so I didn't let him off the hook. "You know my dad, Ed. He's not a criminal. And neither is my mom. And their friends aren't either."

"I never said they were."

"Okay, then."

"But those guys were!"

We spent the next hour not saying much to each other, getting back to work. I shook my head again, this time thinking about myself. I was glad I said something to Ed. But I was glad it didn't make him angrier. Angry enough to fire me. Then again if he did, I guess it would have been okay with me. It was more important for me to tell him what I was thinking about than to keep quiet.

I had to shake my head one more time. Wow, was I changing? At least a little bit? Saying what was on my mind felt good, even if it was a little frightening. I thought of all the other thoughts in my head I was still keeping to myself. About sex, about Bobby, about my family, about being friends with Mr. Aniso, and who knows what else. But all those things together were just too much to think about. *One step at a time, RV,* I told myself, as Mr. Aniso said. *One step at a time.*

*

"Mom, Dad. Why did you come here?"

We were having dinner, and I asked them the question almost as soon as we sat down. With everything I've been thinking about lately, it felt important to find out their answer. Of course we were talking in the Mother Tongue as usual, no English allowed. Only Ray is brave enough to use English at the dinner table. Not me.

Mom and Dad both seemed a little startled, as if the question was strange. Or maybe it was something they haven't thought about in a long time.

But I asked again.

Mom let out a little laugh and said it was so long ago she'd forgotten. Dad looked away. But then Mom began talking about the time Lithuania got its independence in 1990. She said independence was great and people were filled with hope for a better life. She was young and thought things would keep getting better. But, she said, things got worse, much worse for her family. Food was scarce and people had to scrounge for work. Dad chimed in, saying independence comes with a price, maybe a price that's too high for some people.

Mom shook her head. She said the price of independence is never too high. One just has to have patience.

"So you guys didn't have patience?" Ray asked. "That's why you came to the US?"

Mom and Dad looked at each other again. Mom finally answered, shrugging her shoulders. *"Gal neturėjom kantrybės."* "Maybe we did get impatient," she admitted. Then she asked, almost as if asking herself, *"Ar blogai norėti geresnio gyvenimo?"* "Is it wrong to want a better life for yourself?"

Ray and I glanced at each other, not knowing how to answer. Then, to my surprise Dad let out a laugh. But it wasn't a happy laugh. It was a laugh full of anger.

He said Ray and I had no idea what people had to go through to come here. He shook his head, saying he was foolish to think this was the Promised Land. He said it was the land of work and money. If you were lucky or quickly learned how to work the system. But if you didn't, or weren't lucky, it was just work and more work with not much to show for it.

Mom looked like she wanted to say something, but she hesitated. Dad said it for her, saying how the US likes to call itself the land of opportunity. "Ha!" he added dismissively, and said he hadn't found many opportunities, at least not the ones he was hoping for. Then the anger in his eyes turned to sadness and he added that maybe he just didn't know how to look for opportunities.

"But you still believe the opportunities are there for me and RV?" Ray asked in English. "And you still want us to look for them?"

"Taip." "Yes," Mom answered quickly before Dad could say anything.

Ray didn't give up. "What makes you so sure we're any better at finding opportunities than you guys were?"

Mom wouldn't give up either. She reminded Ray that because he and I grew up in this country we were naturally better at it.

Ray looked like he was about to say something snippy, but he kept quiet. But Mom's statement got me thinking. How good was I at finding opportunities? I didn't feel I had any special talent for it. Not compared to someone like Carole, for example, who I'm sure will lead her own company someday.

"So, they want us to find opportunities when they couldn't do it," Ray said when he and I were going up to our rooms after dinner. "Nothing like passing the buck."

"But it's because they want us to have a better life than they did," I said. "It's natural for parents to want that for their kids."

"Yeah, natural and stupid," Ray answered. "Just puts more pressure on us. Without guaranteeing anything."

Chapter Sixteen

On My Own

Well, summer's ending soon and I'm alone. I shouldn't be so dramatic. I feel alone, which is different. My family is still here, but they don't know what I'm going through, so they might as well not exist for me, at least most of the time.

Bobby's not around, not really. I haven't heard from him since we got together at Joe's Pizza and he lectured me about being seen with Mr. Aniso. Yeah, lectured me. I hate to use that word, but that's what it felt like. So, does Bobby really care more about football more than anything else? Including me? Seems like it.

And Carole? What's up with her? We texted each other yesterday. I asked her when she'd be coming home. She told me soon, but didn't give me any details. Then I asked her how she was liking Paris, and she replied with one word, *merveilleux* again. That's it. She did add that she'd tell me all about it when she returned, but she had to rush off somewhere. Well, I'm glad for her. It does sound like she's having a *merveilleux* time and is too busy for her friends back home.

So that just leaves good old Mr. Aniso. But he's busy getting ready for the new school year. He even told me he's got a lot to do because he was out for half the year last year, recovering from his injuries. So was that a hint? Oh, sure, he keeps saying we can get together anytime I want to talk to him, but I don't want to start acting like a crybaby and text him whenever I have the slightest problem or feel bad. He treats me like an adult, at least in some ways, so I want to act like an adult, at least some of the time. LOL.

Oh, RV, stop it. You're starting to feel sorry for yourself again. Things aren't so bad. So, summer hasn't been everything you wanted it to be. But there have been good things, like your friendship with Mr. Aniso. And sophomore year is coming up. Er, excuse me, Class III, as we say in Latin school. You're ready for that, aren't you? And you've finished reading all the assigned books, and more. So whatever essay questions the Class III English teacher is going to throw at you will be a piece of cake, right?

Yeah, I have to admit, books don't scare me. They make me feel good. When I'm reading, I can forget who's here or not here. I'm in some great new world of the book, and I can do anything I want to do. Like the book I'm reading now. My choice, not on any list. *A Distant Mirror.* It's about life in fourteenth-century Europe. It's neat. I like reading about knights and castles. Sometimes I wonder if I was a knight in a previous life.

Oh, who knows about reincarnation, but every time I read about jousting and the battles the knights fought, it all feels so real to me. I can imagine being a knight so easily. Riding on a horse, charging the bad guy coming at me. I'm in white, of course, ha ha, and he's in black since he's the bad guy. Our horses meet, and my lance gets him right in the chest before he gets me. He's down because of my accurate thrust. And I ride off victorious. I love it. And I can really feel it. Crazy, isn't it?

But the book has a lot of interesting history too. Like how people started arguing about religion. Some people disagreed with the Pope in Rome, saying he had become corrupt and bad. So they named someone else Pope in France and said they were following the French Pope because he was the real deal. But the Pope in Rome said no, people had to follow him. He said all the people following the French guy were heretics and were going to hell. But the French Pope said the Italian dude was fake, and people who followed him were going to hell. So people were caught in the middle between the two popes. Who were they supposed to believe?

I'm just glad I don't live in the Middle Ages. Though when I think about it, it's not that different from today, is it? We still argue—a lot. Over everything. And we're still trying to figure out the truth. Like I am about the Big Guy. So I shouldn't make fun of those poor religious schmucks in the fourteenth century. The twenty-first century is pretty crazy too. (Schmucks. Great word. Someone like me, except not so smart, ha ha.)

Wonder what book I should read next. If I want to read anything fun I should do it soon because I'm sure I'll be hit with homework and other reading lists back at school. Not that the books I choose are the only fun ones or have all the answers. But when you do something for school, it becomes another thing you *have* to do. And we have enough of those in life, don't we? Even this summer. Look at all the pressure Bobby's been under. And me too. Maybe that's what those books represent for me. Throwing away all that pressure. Even for a little bit while I'm lost in the book.

*

Well, that's it. I'm done with the computer business. Can't believe what Tim and that curly-head Loretta have been pulling. I ran into Mr. O'Malley this morning. He asked me why I wasn't there to help him with his computer. I didn't know what he was talking about. He was the first guy that Carole and I set up with a computer. I thought everything was going well. But it turns out he was having some problems, trying to install new software or something. It seems Tim and Loretta have been helping him. And not only that, they've done a few other jobs I didn't know about too.

By chance Tim and his buddy Loretta were walking down the street, right after I saw Mr. O'Malley. (Thanks, Big Guy. You're back in the *You Exist, Good Guy* column for the moment.)

I confronted Tim about Mr. O'Malley. He gave me rigmarole (good word, although I can think of some better ones that I wouldn't say at the dinner table). Anyway, Tim gave me some rigamarole about it being a very technical issue so he thought I didn't need to be involved.

"What about the other people you've been helping behind my back?" I asked him.

At first he tried to argue he hadn't gone behind my back. They were all technical issues and I wasn't qualified enough to deal with them.

"And who decides that?" I asked.

No response.

"Loretta is qualified?" I asked again, not letting them off the hook.

Loretta looked a little embarrassed, but she's good at hiding it quickly. "Yes," she said. "My father is a digital engineer. And my mother is a programmer."

"How does that make you qualified?" I demanded.

They didn't answer the question. Tim just said, "Oh, RV. Relax."

I thought of something else. Money. I told them to fork over the money that was due me for all those sessions they had that they didn't tell me about.

Tim said I wasn't due any money because I didn't do any work.

I told him it didn't matter. Carole and I split all work and money evenly. And when Tim came on board it was a split into thirds.

"So where's my third?" I demanded again.

Tim had the gall to ask me where it was written that I get money when I didn't do any work. I had to admit Carole and I had an understanding that all money was split evenly no matter who did the work.

"Understandings don't count in business," Loretta said, looking very high and mighty. "You have to have it written down. That's how business works."

Now she was sounding like Carole. I said something else I'm not proud of and then I turned around and walked away. I texted Carole right away and asked her what was going on. I haven't heard back from her. If she knows about this and she's avoiding me... I better not let myself think that way about Carole or I'll really lose it.

I've got to stop thinking about the computer business, period. It just gets me more pissed off. I'm glad I told off Tim and Loretta. I'm wondering about something else too. Has Tim started going out with Loretta behind Carole's back? If he can go behind my back, he can do it to Carole too. That makes me feel better about Carole, though even worse about Tim.

I better get back to my book. Have to put Tim and Miss Curly-head out of my mind. Besides, when I find out what other crazy things people did to each other in the fourteenth century, it makes me feel a little better about now. One thing is for sure. People haven't changed much at all, have they?

Chapter Seventeen

Making Up

I was very happy—surprised but happy—when Bobby called me today. I tried to play it cool, and our conversation in the beginning was more awkward than anything else.

"Hi, RV."

"Hi, Bobby."

"What's up?"

"Nothing much. What's up with you?"

"Been busy. You know, with football practice and everything. And school starting."

"Yeah, I know. Did you do all your summer reading?"

"No. Did you?"

"Yeah." For a minute I was afraid Bobby would ask me to tell him about the books I read for our Class III summer assignment. Maybe summarize plots or give him notes about the characters, so he'd have a chance to pass whatever test we'll get about them. I've always helped him in the past and, knowing me, I would help him again. Even though this kind of help would be more like cheating, wouldn't it? I'd feel bad about it but would still do it. Bobby really does have me mesmerized, doesn't he?

Luckily, though, Bobby didn't say anything more about our reading assignment. We talked a little more about school starting and who our teachers might be for certain subjects. Then Bobby said he had some free time and asked if I wanted to get together with him.

"Sure," I said, still playing it cool. "I'm not doing much this afternoon."

We agreed to get a slice at Joe's but not eat it there. Instead we'd take the slices to our favorite spot in the woods.

I liked that Bobby said the spot in the woods was "our" favorite, not just "your" favorite, meaning me. That meant he still thought of it as a special place for both of us. I still counted in his life.

I laughed at myself as I was biking over there. Told myself I really liked to read into things, didn't I? Who knows why Bobby said that. Maybe he just said it because I say it. Or it didn't really mean the same thing to him. He's been so up and down lately, it could mean anything. Reminded myself not to pin my hopes on people too quickly.

Am I getting cynical? Good word. Means you don't trust life or other people. I'm not really like that, am I? Hope not. I guess it remains to be seen, as they say.

Bobby and I met at Joe's, got our pizza slices, and went to the woods.

"I've missed this place," Bobby said, as we were sitting on the rock, munching on our pizza.

"I've been coming here a lot," I said. "Anytime I need to think." I had to believe this one spot had still not been discovered by anyone else. Now that Bobby's teammates had started coming to Joe's Pizza, I didn't want to even think about the possibility that someone might find this place too. Ray came close, but not so far.

I looked around as I was finishing my slice. The sun was strong, but it already felt more like fall than summer.

It wasn't humid, and the green hills in the distance stood out sharp and clear against the brilliant-blue sky.

"Life is good, Bobby," I suddenly blurted out. "Being here with you again makes me realize how much I've missed doing this."

I glanced over at Bobby as soon as the words left my mouth. Did he feel the same way? Or would he think I was being too gushy or romantic?

"RV," Bobby said, clearing his throat. "I—I want to apologize."

"Apologize?"

"Yes."

"For what?"

"The last time we got together."

"What about it?"

"I came down a little hard on you about Mr. Aniso."

"Oh, yeah," I nodded. I didn't say anything else. A lot of thoughts were running around my head, and I just waited for what Bobby was going to say next.

"I can see how you and he are good friends and why you like him," Bobby continued. "It just—well, it just spooked me a little."

"You mean the gay thing?"

"Yeah." Bobby cleared his throat again. "I've been thinking about it a lot. And I don't want it to come between us."

Both Bobby and I were not looking at each other as he was saying this. Instead we stared down at the ground or away at the horizon as if making any kind of eye contact was too scary. But now Bobby glanced up at me.

"RV. I've really missed being with you. I miss that more than I'm scared about what people are going to say about me being with you."

"What about the football team? And those coaches you were telling me about?"

"I've been thinking about that too. Being on the team still matters to me. Sure. But I'm good. I know I'm good. And I'll have to mess up real bad if they want to kick me off." He suddenly let out a little laugh. "I guess I learned more at football camp this summer than I thought." He laughed again. "Practice is going well." He turned to me with a determined but shy look on his face. "Those varsity tryouts are coming up, and I'm going to make the team!"

We gave each other high fives.

"Yeah," Bobby said, "if anyone's going to throw me off the team, they better have a good reason."

I wasn't sure what to say. It was good to hear Bobby tell me all that, but I was still worried that if people started to talk more about my being friends with Mr. Aniso, Bobby might change his mind.

I said as much to him. He thought for a second and shook his head. "I promise I won't." My face must have shown the cynical side of RV because he said, "What's the matter, RV? Don't you believe me?"

"I do," I said. But I probably didn't sound very convincing.

"C'mon, RV. You have to believe me." He was staring at me, making it impossible to look away. "You have to trust me."

He got closer, looking into my eyes. Then he suddenly pulled me in close and kissed me on the lips.

He backed off, and we kept staring at each other. "Now do you believe me?" he said in a low voice. "I'm not even worried about who's looking at us now."

I glanced around. "This is the woods. No one's around here."

Bobby shrugged. "Hey, you never know." He reminded me that I had told him about overhearing Ray and his girlfriend nearby. "And seriously," he added, "one thing they kept harping on at football camp was staying positive. That if one play goes bad, you put it out of your mind and concentrate on the next one." He pulled in close to me again. "So I'm staying positive, RV. No matter what happens, my being with you is more important than anything else."

We kissed again. And I couldn't believe this was happening. After everything that had gone wrong this summer.

I promised myself to stay positive too. Whatever the opposite of cynical was, I felt that at the moment. And I was trying my hardest to hold onto it. Because I knew that feeling could go away in an instant.

*

"I feel so much better. Bobby still likes me."

"You saw each other again?"

"Yes. Bobby called and asked if we wanted to get together."

I was at Joe's with Mr. Aniso, telling him about my meeting with Bobby.

"So everything's fine between you two?" Mr. Aniso smiled.

I nodded and then stopped. "Yeah. I mean I think so. I think everything's fine."

I realized I didn't sound very convinced. Mr. Aniso was looking at me, not saying anything, waiting for me to continue.

"Well, I think everything's fine," I repeated. "But—"

"But?" Mr. Aniso leaned forward a little bit, trying to help me along when I hesitated again. "Sounds like there's a 'but' in your mind, RV. What do you think that's all about?"

I told him how Bobby had been worried about my friendship with Mr. Aniso. And how that might affect his being kept on the football team. "He said he didn't care about that anymore. But I guess that's what's bothering me. I don't know if I totally believe him."

"Why do you say that?" Mr. Aniso regarded me sympathetically, which made me feel worse for some reason. "Why do you say that, RV?" he asked again.

"Well, because he cares so much about being on the football team," I finally answered. "And what if... What if something happens and people say something to him? Or worse, what if he gets kicked off the team? Even if it has nothing to do with us, or Bobby being gay, or anything else. I would feel bad. I would feel really bad."

"Yes, that would be bad," Mr. Aniso said, nodding slightly. But then he started shaking his head. "RV, you can't blame yourself for everything."

"I know. But I would. And I wonder if Bobby would, secretly, even if he wouldn't say it."

"There's a lot of prejudice in the world," Mr. Aniso said, nodding again. "And the problem is, we sometimes take on that prejudice."

"What do you mean?" The same dark look I'd seen before transformed Mr. Aniso's face. He sat there quietly, staring off into the distance, like he was remembering something. Something about his life. I was starting to learn there were a lot of things about Mr. Aniso's life I didn't know.

I waited for Mr. Aniso to continue. Now it was my turn to listen and not say anything. Not that I would have known what to say anyway.

But Mr. Aniso didn't seem to be waiting for me to say anything. He was talking again.

"RV, prejudice is very powerful because often it stays hidden, and we ourselves fall victim to it," he was saying. He turned back to me. "I told you about how I missed my friend after I left the seminary. What I didn't tell you was what a bad time it was for me." He stopped again, and thought for a bit, as if making sure whatever he told me was said just the right way. "It was a bad time, a very bad time, and I started to believe that maybe my friend was right in renouncing being gay. So I got angry, and started having sex, and acting out in other ways like drinking a lot. But all that acting out wasn't good because it made me feel bad afterward, not better. I had sex with strangers, sex with people who didn't care about me. Sex that hurt me, and hurt other people too."

He had been looking away as he was telling me this about himself. But now he fixed his gaze on me.

"You see what I was doing, RV? I had taken on everyone else's prejudice, about being gay. And I let the prejudice hurt me too. It took me a long time to learn that's what I was doing and stop hurting myself and other people too." He fell silent for a moment, but then continued. "So, RV. I hope you never do that to yourself. Don't take on other people's prejudices. It's easy to do sometimes, so be careful of that. Like I've always told you, you're a great guy, so please never forget that."

I suddenly felt this wave of love for Mr. Aniso and wanted to jump up and give him a hug. He really cared about me, cared enough that he was sharing painful stuff about his own life so he'd be able to help me.

Just then, Bobby's football friends came into Joe's. Well, it's obvious. My secret pizza place is no secret anymore, if it ever was. Looks like Bobby's teammates like Joe's a lot, and are making it their favorite pizza place just as I and my friends do.

Bobby's teammates glanced at me as they walked by but didn't say anything. The thing was, though, at that moment I didn't really care what they were thinking one way or another. Sitting with Mr. Aniso and talking about our lives seemed more important than anything else. And that felt good. Really good.

*

I'm getting to know my way around hospitals. Melissa's at the same hospital where Mr. Aniso was after he got beat up. I even said hi to Maria, the nurse who took care of him. She remembered me, and gave me a big hug.

"You're becoming a regular here," she said with a laugh.

"I hope not," I said, hugging her back. "I don't like seeing people get hurt."

Ed couldn't close down the garage and gas station, so I went by myself. Even though I said I would be fine, truth is I was a little nervous walking into Melissa's room. You just never know how you're going to find a person when you first see them in a hospital room. You try not to act shocked if they're really bandaged up, but you can't help it. That's how I felt when I saw Mr. Aniso with bandages all over his leg, his side, and even his head. I try not to think what my face looked like then.

Luckily, Melissa seemed fine. The bandages on her stomach were covered up by her nightgown, and she was watching TV and munching on an apple.

"Hey, RV!" she said, extending her arms, wanting to hug me.

I hugged her back, but then she winced. "Oh, I'm sorry," I said. "You have to be careful."

"Yes, yes," she said, looking annoyed. "I have to be careful. Everyone's been telling me that my whole life." She laughed. "Well, I guess I have to listen now." She turned off the TV and motioned for me to sit down by the chair next to her bed. "So, RV. So good to see you. Thanks so much for coming."

"Sure," I replied, a little awkwardly. Though she was getting better, I still wasn't used to Melissa being this friendly to me, hugging me and everything.

A thought occurred to me. "Oh, here. I brought you something," I said, taking out a little box of chocolates I had bought for her. "They told me you can eat anything."

"Oh, RV. You're such a sweetie," Melissa said, taking the chocolates. "Yes, I can eat anything all right. I'm so bored, and can't wait to get back to the garage. So tell me, how's everything there? How's Ed?"

I told her everything was fine, and that Ed was doing okay, though he was busier than usual. "I know he misses you," I said.

Her face darkened a little. "And how are those punks? They haven't come back, have they? Have they been arrested yet?"

I shook my head and told her about the police surveillance. "Having the police there makes everyone feel safer. Me too," I had to admit. "Otherwise my parents wouldn't let me go back there."

Melissa nodded. "I'm sure. It still makes me angry when I think about it. Ed works so hard."

I nodded back but had to ask her a question. "Melissa?" I asked, not quite sure how to begin. "How did you decide to confront those guys? I mean, I was really impressed how brave you were. I—I don't think I'd be that brave."

Melissa shook her head. "I just did it without thinking. It's how I am. If I see something I don't like, I try to correct it." She laughed. "That's how I get myself into trouble sometimes. I act and then I think about it later."

"But—but weren't you scared?"

"Oh, I guess I was scared, but I didn't realize it because it happened so fast." She must have seen I still had a questioning look on my face. "Why do you ask, RV?" she wanted to know.

"Well, because I'm scared sometimes..." It was my turn to laugh. "Ha! Not sometimes, a lot of times. Anyway, when I get scared I clam up and want to hide. Like when my parents are arguing. Or when I saw those guys come into the station. I was glad you came out because I wanted to run away."

"But you didn't," she said. "And you helped Ed take care of me."

"I guess so. That's cuz he was yelling orders at me. If it weren't for him yelling, I think I would have stood there, frozen."

"You don't know if that's true." Then I was surprised because she leaned forward and if I had been sitting close enough she would have grabbed my shoulder the way Mr. Aniso did that time I visited him in the hospital. "RV," she said. "Learn to give yourself the benefit of the doubt. You're a great guy. And you don't know how you'd react until you're in that situation." She smiled. "And you never know. Maybe you will be in that kind of situation someday. And then you'll see how you react. And I bet you will be great. And brave."

Brave. What a big word. I've never associated it with myself. Nice of Melissa to say it, though. I guess she's right. You never know what life will throw at you. Ha! I don't want to think about that. Not now. Because the thought of acting like Melissa did with the punks scares me. But with Mr. Aniso and now Melissa telling me how brave and how great I am, who knows? Maybe someday I'll really believe it.

Chapter Eighteen

Ceremony

Well, after all that, the arguments and studying and worrying, Mom and Dad became citizens. They had their interview today and they passed with flying colors. Ahem, Dad passed with flying colors. Mom did just okay. At least that's what they told me.

The woman interviewing them gave Dad really easy questions. Well, that's according to Mom, anyway. Mom says she got harder ones: name three current justices of the Supreme Court. And name the next four people who would succeed the President if he were killed or incapacitated. Gee, I know the next three—the Vice President, the Speaker of the House, and President of the Senate (I think)—but the fourth one? The President's wife? Ha ha. I should google that.

Anyway, I'm really happy too. Now there will be one less reason for Mom and Dad to argue. And one less reason for Dad to threaten to go back to the Old Country.

I tried to examine Dad's face when he came back from the interview. Couldn't tell how happy he was or if he was happy at all. At least he didn't say anything negative. So for Dad maybe that's positive.

Mom, of course, was very happy. She got on the phone with a couple of friends and told them about the interview. She giggled, talking about what she was going to wear for the swearing-in ceremony. And then she called her friend Myrna from work, the friend with whom she was going to go into business. Apparently Myrna has changed her mind again and now she says she can come up with some money for their jewelry business.

So Myrna and Mom are back working together again. They have already started negotiations on a lease in some building downtown. Mom knows she'll have to work longer hours to make a little more money to put into the business, but she seems excited about it. Good for her. And good for her for spreading some good cheer around. And good for this family to have something positive happen for a change. I just hope the good vibes stay a while.

*

So I was sitting on my favorite rock at my favorite place. Needed to get energized, which I guess is what I do there. Not that I was feeling particularly down. Even though summer's ending, I'm not as sad as I thought I'd be. I'm happy about Mom and Dad becoming citizens. I'm happy that Mr. Aniso and I are friends. I'm happy that Melissa is doing better. And I'm actually looking forward a little to sophomore year. I turned fifteen at the beginning of the summer, and I guess I feel like I've learned a lot in the past three months.

Sure, I wish Bobby and I had more time together, but most of the time we've had is good. And about being gay, well, I still have a bunch of questions about all that, but Mr. Aniso keeps assuring me the answers will come in time. So I have to believe him. He's helped me in so many other ways, I trust him on this too.

I was sitting there on the rock, thinking about all these things and watching the sun go down behind the hills. Maybe that's why I was feeling good too. I like evenings. At that time of day, the sun makes the sky look golden-orange, and if there are a few clouds in the sky they really light up when the sun is setting. And then the evening sounds start: the cricket noises and the other gentle sounds in the trees. The world is getting into its quiet, peaceful phase. And all your tasks for the day are finished. (Or should be finished!) I could stay in those moments forever.

Except good old life never lets you relax for too long, does it? It didn't stay quiet very long as I started hearing voices and laughter. Oh, sure. It was Ray and his friends again, I was sure of it. Ray has that distinctive laugh I can tell from far away. Except it wasn't far away. And it was getting closer.

And suddenly there was Ray bursting through the trees followed by his friends. Great. I've accepted that my favorite pizza place has been discovered. Is my rock not mine anymore too? I guess that's something else I've learned this summer. I have to find new RV hangouts.

Ray and friends stopped short when they saw me. There were two other guys I didn't recognize and a girl. She was the first one who spoke.

"Oh, hi," she said giggling. "We didn't mean to intrude."

Yup. She was the one I had heard with Ray that other time. Was she his girlfriend?

"Hi, Ray," I said.

"Hi." He looked embarrassed to see me. I noticed the cigarette in his hand. At least it wasn't a joint. I was relieved to see a couple of his other friends had cigarettes and not joints in their hands too. I couldn't help shaking my head, though. What's the world come to when you're happy your baby brother is smoking cigarettes instead of something worse?

We all stayed like that, staring at each other without saying anything for a minute or two.

Then the girl spoke up again, giggling. "Nice sunset. We didn't mean to disturb you. We'll find our own place to watch it."

With that she turned around and went back through the trees, the boys following her.

I stayed there for a while longer, trying to compose myself and watch the sun go completely behind the hills. But I couldn't relax. Thinking about Ray just bothers me. I know he has his own life, and if he doesn't want to confide in me that's his problem. Why should I care? There are a lot of brothers who don't get along. Why should we be any different?

But I couldn't let it go. Cigarettes are better than joints, but still they're not great for a kid of his age. And who knows if Ray and his friends still don't smoke joints?

I felt like such a nerdy, protective older brother. But I had to say something. I went home and waited for him to get home too.

"So, you discovered my hiding place," I said, walking into his room.

He looked kind of sheepish. "Yeah, sorry about that," he said. "We didn't mean to."

"I know."

He looked at me with a pleading look in his eyes. "You're not going to tell Mom and Dad you saw me, are you?"

"You mean smoking?"

"Yeah."

"I told you before I wouldn't, but I just might have to," I added, after hesitating for a second.

"We just smoke occasionally," Ray said, as if that was an excuse for me not saying anything to Mom and Dad. "And we have a good time together."

"The last time you were smoking pot."

"We switched to cigarettes."

"Those aren't great, either," I said, not sure whether I believed him or not, anyway. I took a breath and launched into my spiel. "Ray, I told you I won't say anything," I repeated. "But I'm worried about you. I don't want you to get into worse trouble. Or ruin your health." Boy, how did that come across? But I had to say it.

Ray, of course, wasn't buying it. "Don't worry, I can take care of myself."

"Mom and Dad would be devastated if something seriously bad happened to you," I said, ignoring him.

Ray snorted. "Ha. Like what? Like me going to jail? Getting lung cancer?"

"Ray, it's not a joking matter."

"I know it isn't. So stop saying stupid things."

"What's stupid about what I'm saying?"

"Nothing. Just get off my back."

"Look, I know living with Mom and Dad isn't easy sometimes. But it's not that bad."

"Stop making excuses for them! You don't even know how it feels following their rules and watching them argue, and being a good Lith and going to Lith mass and going to school on Saturdays. You're lucky, you like being a good kid!"

"I do not!"

"Oh, yes, you do! You don't even know it, but you do! And you have no idea how it feels if you don't want to be a good kid!"

Ray was staring at me with a deep anger in his eyes. It scared me.

"So lay off me!" he continued. "I hate the things you love! And I hate that you don't get that about me! Just like Mom and Dad don't get it!"

I didn't think I loved being a good kid, but maybe it was easier for me than for Ray. I wanted to say more, but the anger in Ray's eyes showed me it would be useless, at least today.

Ray realized I was retreating from the room. So he gave me one last parting shot.

"So if you want to be the good guy and follow the rules, go ahead and do it! Because I don't. It's not my life and it never will be! You hear me. It never will be!"

I left Ray's room like I'd done all the times before. Not having a clue about how to get through to him. The gulf between us seemed to be getting bigger and bigger.

What I hate most about it, I guess, is that I feel whatever I say or do will just make things worse and piss Ray off even more. So is that another lesson I have to learn? There are some bad things you just have to learn to live with?

If it is, it's a hard one. And I wish I didn't have to learn it.

*

Well, what a day. The naturalization ceremony. Ray didn't want to go at first but then he agreed. So we both went with Mom and Dad. It was held in a hall at the JFK Library, the presidential library dedicated to President

John F. Kennedy. It's a modern, mostly white building on Boston Harbor. I love the view over the harbor and the Boston skyline in the distance. The day was beautiful, sunny but not too hot. Mom and Dad promised that after the ceremony we could walk by the water and relax in the park that was on the grounds too.

Mom and Dad both looked a little nervous, walking into the building. But happy too. I felt like a parent, taking his kids to graduation. A little weird, but a good feeling. A new life for them, I guess.

The ceremony was more interesting than I expected. First a judge welcomed everyone. She said there were more than two hundred people getting their citizenship that day from thirty-two different countries. She mentioned all the countries one by one and asked everyone from that country to stand up when their country was called. When it was Lithuania's turn, Mom and Dad stood up. They had been given little US flags when they walked into the hall, and they looked so cute standing and waving their flags, like little kids with their precious new toys.

After all the countries were announced and everyone was standing, it was time for the oath of allegiance. Most people placed their hands over their hearts, including Mom and Dad. The oath began, *"I hereby declare, on oath, that I absolutely and entirely renounce and abjure all allegiance and fidelity to any foreign prince, potentate, state, or sovereignty..."* And it continued with a lot of other serious-sounding words about being loyal to the United States and upholding its laws.

I looked at Mom and Dad's faces and wondered what they were thinking as they were standing there with their hands over their hearts. Was Dad thinking about his own father who had died protesting occupation by the Russians? Or his brother who was "on the other side" back home, whatever that meant? And what about Mom? Was she thinking about her new business she was going to start with her friend, Myrna? Or the business that failed last spring where she lost money? Was she worried? Was Dad sad? I couldn't tell. Whatever their thoughts were, they were very private.

When the oath was finished a congressman was introduced to give the main talk. He said he was naturalized, too, having come here from Brazil. He welcomed all the new citizens, saying now they were free to enjoy all the freedoms and rights of the United States. "Look at me," he joked. "I can't be president, but I'm now a congressman who's fighting for a better country in Washington. And who knows what I can accomplish in the future. Life in Washington isn't easy, but it's worth it."

But then he turned serious, saying with rights there are responsibilities. And he asked everyone to vote, saying "this country might not be perfect, but the preamble to the Constitution says we strive to be a more perfect union." He paused and gazed over at everyone. "We strive," he repeated. "We're not perfect, but we try, that's what striving means."

"And one way to strive is by voting," he emphasized. "By voting you, too, can do your part for yourselves, your children, and all the immigrants who come after you and keep the American Dream alive. So vote. Please vote and do your part in making this country even greater than it is. Remember, the word is strive. We all strive together."

Everyone applauded and there were tears on some people's faces. I looked at Dad again, and he quickly wiped a tear from his face. I turned my head away because I know he didn't want anyone to see him cry. Dad, cry? Crying at the family dinner table was dramatic enough. But in public? Well, there's a first time for everything, right?

And then it was time for the reason everyone was there. They gave out the certificate of naturalization. Everyone was called one by one by the congressman and they went up in a line to get their certificate. There were some real tongue twister names in the group. I held my breath when it was time for Mom and Dad's names. Dad always complains that people mispronounce our name. "Aleksandravičius." What's so hard about that? Duh, Dad. Why don't you try to say Ahunna Igbinedion? Or Vasilios Papageorgiou? Or Xixellore Haradinaj?

The congressman must have really practiced because he got Mom and Dad's names right, though he stumbled over a few other names. Did he really spend time going over all two hundred names? Maybe he's right. Life in Washington isn't really as easy as we think.

After all the certificates were handed out it was time for the national anthem. I don't know, I don't like our national anthem. First of all the notes are so high in places, I end up squeaking a lot of lines, just like many people did today. And then it's about war and bombardment. Yeah, yeah, we have to defend our country, but couldn't it be about something else? Opportunity? Immigration? Being free? Pursuing life, liberty, and happiness? Isn't that in the Constitution too? Though how you write a song about that, I don't know.

After the ceremony was done everyone went outside to take pictures, look at the view over the harbor, and congratulate each other. I took Mom and Dad's picture. Then we took other people's pictures and they offered to take all four of us together. There all four of us are in the pictures, smiling and happy, even Ray. Mom and Dad are smiling most of all, holding up their little flags and certificates.

I asked them how they felt.

"Mes esam Amerikonai! Valio!" Mom said with a cheer. "We're Americans! Bravo!"

Mom poked Dad in the ribs and got him to hold up his flag and say *"Valio!"*, too, so I could take another picture. Dad's smile was almost as broad as Mom's. It was so nice to see he was happy after all the stress of the citizenship process.

It felt good. We felt like a real family. At least today.

*

After we came home, I googled the entire oath you have to take when you become a citizen.

> *I hereby declare, on oath, that I absolutely and entirely renounce and abjure all allegiance and fidelity to any foreign prince, potentate, state, or sovereignty, of whom or which I have heretofore been a subject or citizen; that I will support and defend the Constitution and laws of the United States of America against all enemies, foreign and domestic; that I will bear true faith and allegiance to the same; that I will bear arms on behalf of the United States when required by the law; that I will perform noncombatant service in the Armed Forces of the United States when required by the law; that I will perform work of national importance under civilian direction when required by the law; and that I take this*

obligation freely, without any mental reservation
or purpose of evasion; so help me God."

Hmmm. I don't know what to think. There's still a lot about war and fighting there, though I can see the point of that. But I also like the part about performing work of national importance. There are a lot of things we can do to make this country better. What should mine be?

Chapter Nineteen

Being a Man

I knew Bobby would be busy, but I guess I didn't realize how busy. School's starting and I haven't seen him since we had our talk and kissed on the rock last week. Was it just last week? Early last week, so more than seven days has passed.

I hope I'm not getting sad and jealous. Like those football widows they talk about. Or one of those girly girls whose crush is not being returned. I have to believe Bobby meant what he said. He doesn't worry about being seen with me or people seeing me with Mr. Aniso. He said I'm more important to him than that, right? I even asked him if he really meant that, didn't I? And he said yes, didn't he?

So why do I still have my doubts? Is this another one of those life lessons I'm supposed to learn? If you like someone and want to be with them, they might not want to be with you at the same time. It's not that they're rejecting you. It's that their schedule is different from yours. After all, their life is different from yours too. Didn't Mr. Aniso say that? I believe everything else he told me, so I should believe this too. Right?

Maybe. Let me take the Fifth Amendment on that, or whatever amendment it is. I don't know how I feel about it, and don't want to incriminate myself any further. I'll know how my friendship with Bobby is going as the school year progresses, with or without football.

And I finally got a proper text from Carole. With real information and not just saying how *merveilleux* everything is. She's coming home next week. I'll finally get the lowdown on Tim and the computer business (Whose computer business is it now, anyway? Carole's and Tim's? Carole's, Tim's, and Loretta's? Tim's and Loretta's?). One thing's for sure. It's certainly not mine anymore. Carole will tell me the truth, won't she?

Yes, I want to hear about Paris, too. Yes, it was "*merveilleux!*" as Carole keeps saying. My summer hasn't quite been *maravilloso*, but it's been pretty good. Here's a new game for you, Carole. We try to communicate with you talking only in French, and me in Spanish. And no Tim, because he only talks computerese. How's that sound?

I've started to think about all the good stuff that will happen sophomore year. It's a good sign. I'm being positive, and not cynical, ha ha. Maybe that's the most important thing I learned this summer. Think about the future. Don't rush things. Look forward to the classes you enjoy, like English and History. And don't think about the bad ones. You'll get Carole to help you. And look forward to finding another pizza joint since Joe's has become too popular. (Good luck with that!)

Oh, and one more thing. Look forward to Mom and Dad being citizens. Will they act any different? Who knows? But after all that worrying and arguing, they're now full citizens of the USA. Miracles happen, ha ha. So things will work out for me and Bobby right?

*

Well, there it goes. Life is doing its thing again. Showing me something unexpected. Good stuff. Just good stuff I never thought about. Not much anyway.

Mr. Aniso texted me. Yes, he texted me! Not the other way around. He asked to see me at Joe's for a slice of pizza. Said he wants to wish me good luck for the coming school year. And he also said he wants me to meet someone.

Well, that's interesting. Who could that be? Someone he met? Another friend? Someone else gay? From school? Am I ready for that? Why am I nervous? I should be excited. I am excited. But nervous, too. Okay, *calm down, RV!* Just chill out and go meet Mr. Aniso. He's always given you good advice, so don't be nervous. Just say yes and let the excited part take over the nervous part. After all it's a new school year and new things are going to happen. Didn't you just tell yourself to look forward to the future and enjoy it?

*

I made sure I got to Joe's early. I don't know what it is, but I hate walking into anyplace late. Meeting friends, or a class at school, or anything. Makes me nervous. Is that a weakness or just one of those RV things? Who knows?

I was glad not too many people were at Joe's. Glad, too, I didn't see any of Bobby's football friends. Have to admit, that would make me even more nervous, even though I said it wouldn't matter to me anymore.

So I got a slice and a Coke and sat down in one of the booths, waiting for Mr. Aniso. Took out my phone and pretended to relax. Another text from Carole! She gave me her flight number and other details. Great! We'll have so much to talk about.

"Hi, RV."

Mr. Aniso was standing there with another guy next to him.

"Oh, hello," I said, trying to stand up in the booth, but banging my knee against the table.

Awkwardly, I stuck out my hand. "RV, this is Ben," Mr. Aniso said. "Ben, this is my friend, RV."

"Hello," both Ben and I said to each other, shaking hands.

"Well, let's get some pizza," Mr. Aniso said to Ben. He turned to me. "Need anything?"

I shook my head, happy to sit down again.

They went up to the counter to order their slices. Ben was about Mr Aniso's age. He looked like a librarian, short and skinny, and with big, wide glasses and dark hair that made him look studious. Yeah, a real librarian. Or a professor.

They got their slices and drinks, and sat back down in the booth.

"So, RV," Mr. Aniso said, "are you looking forward to sophomore year?"

"Yeah," I nodded. "Though it's going to be hard. I have to take chemistry, and I don't know how good I am in that."

"You're studious. I'm sure you'll do fine," Mr. Aniso said.

"Thanks," I said. "I'm continuing with my Spanish and Latin. Reading *Julius Caesar* next year. I'm not sure about reading in Latin, but I like history." I mentioned the book about the fourteenth century that I almost finished reading.

"I'm impressed," Ben said. "Reading that on your own. Great." He winked at me. "And don't knock Latin. Not in front of Mr. Aniso."

We all laughed.

We sat there for a few minutes, just eating our pizza and enjoying the moment, not saying anything. Mr. Aniso finally broke the silence. He said, "RV, Ben is a friend of mine. I met him in rehab at the hospital."

"Oh?"

"Yes. He had injured himself in a bike accident, so he had to do physical therapy for that."

"Oh," I said again. "I like biking too. But yeah, you have to be careful. Are you better now?" I asked Ben.

Ben nodded. "Mostly. My knee is a little dicey, so I'm still doing therapy. But I should be fully recovered soon."

We sat there quietly again, eating our pizza slices. "Um, RV," Mr. Aniso said, breaking the silence again. He looked a little nervous. That surprised me. I'd never seen Mr. Aniso nervous, at least not with me. "RV, Ben is more than a friend of mine. We're dating."

"Oh, that's great," I said, not knowing what else to say.

"Yes, I feel lucky to have met Charlie," Ben said. "He's a great guy."

I was nodding, but thinking about Mr. Aniso being called Charlie. Funny. In all this time, I don't think I ever knew his first name. He's always been Mr. Aniso to me.

"That's great," I repeated, feeling a little nervous myself. Here I was meeting someone Mr. Aniso was dating. It was a little odd, since it was the first time I was in this situation, meeting someone a gay person was dating. But I felt flattered Mr. Aniso told me yet another personal thing.

I just wished I could think of something intelligent to say. Then it came to me. "Mazeltov!" Isn't that what people say when good things happen?

That broke the awkwardness. We all laughed. Mr. Aniso raised his Coke cup.

"Mazeltov!"

Ben raised his. "Mazeltov!"

And I raised mine. "Mazeltov!"

"See, I told you, Ben," Mr. Aniso said. "In addition to being a great guy, RV is smart. Great with languages."

"Wait till I get my chemistry and math grades this year," I said, laughing. "If they're okay, then you can say something like that."

We started talking more freely. Mr. Aniso told me that Ben was a librarian at the Boston Public Library. Aha! I was right!

I told Ben I'd like to visit him there as I liked to look at microfilm of old newspapers.

"Then you're in luck!" Ben said. "That's the department where I work."

I was genuinely excited. I told them I liked finding out how old newspapers reported current events, like the sinking of the *Titanic* or the moon landing in 1969 or the Boston Red Sox winning the World Series in 2004.

"Come anytime," Ben said. "We have a ton of old newspapers."

Wow. What a great afternoon at Joe's. Mr. Aniso and Ben told me some more about the things they did together this summer like going to the Fourth of July concert on the Esplanade and spending a weekend in Cape Cod. I told them a little bit about my summer too. Told them about working in the garage, and missing Carole, and spending time with Bobby. I paused before mentioning Bobby's name, still feeling bad about the time he got mad at me for telling Mr. Aniso he might be gay. This time I just mentioned him as a friend, which he is. Is he more than a friend, though? Funny how these things can trip you up.

But at the moment I didn't care. It was great talking to Mr. Aniso and Ben as friends, sharing our summer experiences. I was so glad Mr. Aniso had brought Ben along. The more I talked to him, the more comfortable I felt.

I already consider Mr. Aniso a friend. And now maybe Ben will become one too.

*

Finally!

Bobby called this morning. The day before school starts.

"Hey, RV," he said. "No football practice. So we have one free day of summer before school starts. Do you want to get together?"

It's the same old story. If Bobby wants to get together, do I ever say no? Will I ever stop being mesmerized by him? I hope not. I'm starting to accept that being mesmerized is part of life too. It's just how you deal with it that matters.

Bobby and I came up with a great idea. Going to back Larz Anderson Park to say goodbye to summer. We went there at the beginning of the summer, and we both thought we'd get there more often. That didn't work out so well, did it? Hard to believe we never went back there. But that's life, right, RV? Another one of your wonderful lessons.

So we biked over there this afternoon. It was hot. Hotter than when we were there at the beginning of summer. But I did okay, keeping up with Bobby. Glad I brought all that water along.

There weren't many people on the hill because the sun was so strong and there was no breeze. But I was glad our special area in the trees was empty. Had no one else really discovered it? Didn't really matter, did it? We were just happy it was empty today.

It was hazy day, so the skyline of Boston wasn't very visible. We didn't mind. We found our old spot under the big tree where it was shady and a little cooler. It was nice just to sit and be quiet and pretend the world was far away.

"I'm—I'm glad you called, Bobby," I said a little hesitantly after a while. "I know you've been busy with practice, but I was beginning to think I wouldn't see you at all before school started."

Bobby nodded. "I know. I'm sorry. It really has been a little crazy."

He paused and looked at me. His eyes were blazing, and he looked like he was about to burst.

"I have some news," he said.

"News?"

"I made the team. I made the varsity football team!"

"What?"

"Yes!"

"Fantastic!" I threw my around him and gave him a huge hug. "I'm so happy for you."

He laughed. "I'm happy for me too. After all that work. And the fights with my dad..."

He let go of me and started frowning with the memories. I frowned too.

"Are we going to have any time to get together?" I asked him. "Look what happened this summer."

"I know. I'm sorry, and I know a lot of it is my fault," said Bobby. "But I'll try. I'll really try." He turned to me. "You know how important making the varsity team is for me, RV."

I nodded. We both sat there silently for a bit. Then Bobby spoke. "And if I get nervous about Mr. Aniso, forgive me in advance." He turned to me again. "Just remember, being a player in the football world is so different from the regular world. Your world."

"What's so different about my world?" I asked.

"Well, there's the gay stuff," Bobby said.

"But...but you said you might be gay too?"

"I know. But you're more out than me."

"Out? That's a laugh. I see Mr. Aniso and now his friend, Ben. And that's it."

"That's more than me." He looked away, and I could tell this was one of those don't-interrupt-Bobby moments because he'd got something important on his mind.

So I sat and waited until he finally spoke again.

"It's not just being gay. I'm learning something else in football practice."

"What?"

"It's a different way of thinking. And being a man."

"Being a man?"

"Yeah. You know, the discipline part. The being strong part. The succeeding part. I have to admit I like that. Maybe I'm more like my father than I want to admit. I do want to prove something to the world."

"So?"

"So, I look at Mr. Aniso, and he doesn't seem to care about proving anything to anyone."

"Yeah, I know. He may not look macho or strong, but he's certainly strong inside, like I've said."

"Yeah, that's just it. I don't know if I can be like that. I want to be strong on the inside and outside too," Bobby continued. "Is that bad of me?

"I don't think so," I told him. "That's who you are. A man can be strong in a lot of ways."

"Yeah, I guess so."

Bobby was thinking and turned to me, asking, "RV. What do you consider a man?"

I couldn't help it, but I laughed. "Oh, Bobby, I'm still trying to figure out myself. I'll worry about what a man is after I figure out being a teenager!" I turned to him, becoming a little more serious. "You know, Mr. Aniso is always telling me not to rush things. He says take one step at a time, and the future will take care of itself."

I was glad Bobby was smiling, even though he was shaking his head. "Yeah, I guess you're right, RV. I worry too much about the future. Even my father said that. But he's the one who worries about the future too much. The other day he asked me if I'd like to work for the Mooch again next summer."

"What did you tell him?"

"I told him to lay off. And we had a fight."

We both shook our heads. "Yeah, adults can be pretty ignorant sometimes."

"Sometimes? A lot of the time!" Bobby said. He turned, put his arms around me, and gave me a tight hug. "Oh, RV. Good old Mr. Aniso is right. Let's forget about the future. Today we need to celebrate."

"Yes, we do! We gotta think of something cool to do."

Bobby laughed. "We will. Hey," he added. "I know you're not a big football fan, but you'll come to watch me play for Latin occasionally?"

"Sure. And now maybe I'll become a fan."

Bobby gave me another hug, and I put my arms around him. We sat there under the tree, closing our eyes and holding each other for who knows how long.

When I opened them I saw the late-afternoon haze had cleared a bit and there were more people on the hillside.

"It's going to be a nice evening," I said.

Bobby nodded. He pointed to the Boston skyline in the distance.

"Yeah, you can see the buildings more clearly now. And those lights twinkling in the buildings. Don't they look so cute? Like they're talking to us."

"Wow. Who's the poet now?" I said, laughing. "You see? The future has taken care of itself. Without our worrying about it."

Bobby laughed too. "That's another thing I like about you, RV. Besides helping me with homework, you'll show me how to think about life."

Me knowing how to think about life? That was about the dumbest thing Bobby had ever said. But if it was going to make him happy, who was I to say no?

Then we sat there, just holding each other. We stayed there till the lights in Boston came on everywhere, glowing brightly, and we got that same bit of magic we had at the beginning of summer.

All too soon it was time to go home and face our parents. But that was okay. I knew real life would be back ASAP and I'm sure Bobby and I will have a zillion questions again tomorrow and learn more hard lessons. But I guess that's what it's all about, right?

About the Author

Andy V. Roamer grew up in the Boston area and moved to New York City after college. He worked in book publishing for many years, starting out in the children's and YA books division and then wearing many other hats. This is his second novel about RV, the teenage son of immigrants from Lithuania in Eastern Europe, as RV tries to navigate his demanding high school, his budding sexuality, and new relationships. He has written an adult novel, *Confessions of a Gay Curmudgeon*, under the pen name Andy V. Ambrose. To relax, Andy loves to ride his bike, read, watch foreign and independent movies, and travel.

Email: andyvroamer@gmail.com

Facebook: www.facebook.com/andyvroamer

Instagram: www.instgram.com/andy_v_roamer

Website: www.thepizzachronicles.com

Other NineStar books by this author

Why Can't Life Be Like Pizza?

Coming Soon from Andy V. Roamer

Why Can't Relationships Be Like Pizza?

I thought sophomore year would be easier. I got through freshman year okay, even got an award for good grades and good behavior. Yeah, I'm such an angel. It'll take a long time to live that down. Whalen is in my home room again. Hope he's over drawing pictures of his classmates, especially me. If he only knew the real me, maybe he wouldn't have drawn that halo over my head.

Anyway, sophomore year sure isn't starting out any easier. I can already tell my Chemistry class is going to be no picnic. I'm a right-brain guy, creative and nerdy, ha ha, not analytical and nerdy. And too bad I don't have Mr. Aniso for Latin class this year. It would great reading *Julius Caesar* with him, wouldn't it? Better than having Latin with Miss Wagstaff. Reminds me of a librarian crossed with some of our nuns in grammar school. She's tall and skinny with tight curly hair and these round granny glasses that make her eyes look huge. She never smiles, and when she gets mad, her eyes get bigger behind those glasses, her arms fly around, and she starts to screech like one of those scary prehistoric birds. Oh, for the days of Mr. Aniso.

And this year's Math teacher, Mr. Felucci, never smiles either. He's strict too. Reminds me of a mean, fat army sergeant who likes to put you on the spot in class. Not fun for my right-sided brain.

At least there's Señorita Sanchez, our Spanish teacher. She's from Spain and so gorgeous, even I might start to have fantasies about her. She's tough, too, but nice about it. Doesn't make us feel bad if we get something wrong.

So school's not all bad, right? I guess not. But it's my life that's—what?—kind of somewhere out there in some crazy zone, not exactly where I want it to be. Especially where my friends are concerned. Most importantly Bobby. I still think we're close, aren't we? We did have that nice talk in our favorite place in the woods, where he apologized and said he still cared about me. I'm so happy for him. He was so excited about making the varsity football team.

But guess what? I haven't seen him since then. Not alone anyway. He's not in any of my classes. Oh, I see him in the corridors at school, where he's nice to me, like he's nice to everybody. That's what makes him so great. Mr. Nice Guy, despite being a jock and making the varsity football team. He could be so full of himself, though he's not. He's just busy with school and practice. Always practice. So friends have to take second place. Is that how it works?

Also Available from NineStar Press

Connect with NineStar Press

www.ninestarpress.com

www.facebook.com/ninestarpress

www.facebook.com/groups/NineStarNiche

www.twitter.com/ninestarpress